U0094026

哈福

學英語，像學１２３一樣簡單

# 輕鬆學會

## American
## Talks Made Easy

# 美國口語

## 美國人一天到晚說的話

## 3分鐘學會，一輩子受益

附 MP3

蘇盈盈 —— 著

FRESH JUICE

哈福

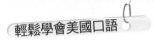

# 用美國口語，和老外聊不停

英語老是學不會嗎？碰到老外，很想説！？不會説！？説不出口！？快翻開本書，英語立即脱口説！62 句嗆辣美國口語，馬上可以和老美溜英語，輕輕鬆鬆説美式英語。

輕鬆學會美國口語，都是老美一天到晚説的話，3 分鐘學會，一輩子受益，升學、求職、旅遊、貿易，無往不利，英語流利脱口説。

## 學美語，就像學 123 一樣簡單

‧Anytime.（隨時歡迎。）‧Be my guest.（請便。）‧Beats me.（這可難倒我了。）‧Drop it!（別再説了。）‧Not again.（別又來了。）‧No way.（免談；不會的。）‧Suit yourself.（隨便你。）‧Look who's here.（看誰來了。）

夠嗆吧！你看是不是很簡單，每個單字、每個句子，都很簡單、都很迷你，都是你早就學過，每一句都是最常説的美國口語，超簡單、超好學，秒學秒會，擁有本書，保證你輕鬆和老美溜英語。

## 跟上潮流，學好英語

學英語的好處很多：除了可以開拓自己的眼界、結交更多朋友、獲得多元的第一手消息、瀏覽網站更方便之外，影響我們最大的，無非是精通英語在職場上佔盡了優勢！想進入各大國際公司，説得一口漂亮的英語更是必備的基礎技能！

英語能力除了讀與寫，最直接的便是口説與聽力。能説一口漂亮的英語，第一印象就加了許多分，可説是開啟了在公司平步青雲，

扶搖直上的第一扇門了！

 ## 說英語時，不要想中文

　　我常說要講一口流利的英語，最重要的是，說英語的時候，腦子裡不可以想中文，腦子裡要用英語去想，如果，你先想中文再把所想的翻譯成英語，那麼你說出來的英語一定是「台客英語」。

　　換句話說，雖然你滿嘴英語，其實你是在說中文，那樣的英語，老美是聽不懂的。要怎麼樣才能夠在說英語的時候，不要想中文，直接想英語呢？最有效的方法就是帶個老美回家，每天跟著他說英語，我知道，在台灣的環境，哪有可能這麼奢侈，帶個老美回家，天天跟他說英語。

## 每一句，都是美國人每天說的英語

　　所以，美國 **AA Bridgers** 公司為了幫助大家學好英語，組了一群美國人，天天集思廣益的在模擬美國的生活，美國人每天說的話，製作成一套套的英語學習書，我們分成各類來教，有的是以基礎句型來作為學習的藍本，有的模擬日常生活，本書則是以教美國口語為主，這些話，都是美國人一天到晚說的英語。

　　我們為了讓您的學習過程，如同請個老美在你身邊一樣，每本書都有請美國老師錄音，你如果能夠天天一有空，就播放這些美國人錄音的 MP3，跟著唸，當你說英語時，就可以輕鬆開口溜出來，和老美聊不停，而不需要先想中文怎麼說，再把所想的翻譯成英語。

　　如能做到這樣，把英文當母語，說英文像說中文，那麼，碰到老外，你就能用英語聊不停了！

# *Part 1* 美國口語開口說

CONTENTS 目錄

CONTENTS 目錄

## Part 2 實用會話練習

# PART

# 1

# 美國口語開口說

# 1 Anytime.

### 隨時歡迎

輕鬆學 你幫了別人的忙,對方跟你道謝,你可以回答 Any time. 表示說,對方可以隨時來請你幫忙,你都會很樂意幫她的。

對話 一

A : Thanks for picking up my daughter after school yesterday.

B : Anytime.

> A:謝謝你昨天放學時接我女兒。
> B:隨時歡迎你來找我。

對話 二

A : I appreciate your helping me paint the fence. I couldn't have finished it alone.

B : Don't worry about it. Anytime.

> A:謝謝你幫我油漆籬笆。我自己做不完的。
> B:別擔心這個。隨時歡迎你來找我。

## 加 強 練 習

| | |
|---|---|
| **pick up**<br>接人 | I'm going to pick Mary up at the airport.<br>（我要去機場接瑪麗。）<br><br><br>Could you pick up my daughter after school today?<br>（今天我女兒放學後你可以去接她嗎？） |
| **finish**<br>完成 | Are you finished reading the newspaper?<br>（你報紙看完了嗎？）<br><br>Have you finished your homework yet?<br>（你的功課做完了嗎？） |

☐ appreciate    [əˈpriʃɪˌet]      動 感激

☐ paint    [pent]      油漆

☐ fence    [fɛns]      籬笆

☐ finish    [ˈfɪnɪʃ]      完成

☐ alone    [əˈlon]      形 單獨的；獨自

☐ worry    [ˈwɝɪ]      動 憂慮；擔心

**Memo**

## 2 **Beats me.**

這可難倒我了。

MP3-3

**輕鬆學** beat 這個字可以做「打敗」的意思，有人提出你也不知道答案的問題，例如：大家約好了要見面，時間到了，卻不見約翰出現，有人不禁要問，約翰怎麼啦，為什麼沒來啊，你也不知道約翰為什麼沒有到，你就可以回答說 Beats me. 也就是說對方這個問題把你難倒了的意思。這句話完整的說法是 It beats me. 這句話裡的「it」就是對方問的話，雖然說話時「it」這個字常常可以省略掉，但是 beat 還是得加 s.

**對話 一**

A : I wonder where John is.

He was supposed to meet us an hour ago.

B : Beats me.

He's never late.

A：我在想約翰不知道在哪裡。他一個小時之前就該來跟我們碰面的。

B：我不知道。他從不遲到的。

15

## 對話 二

A ： What's wrong with the copy machine?

It's been acting up all day.

B ： Beats me.

I don't know anything about electronics.

A：影印機怎麼啦？這一整天都沒辦法正常運轉。

B：這可難倒我了。我對電子的東西是一竅不通。

## 加 強 練 習

---

**wonder**
想要知道

I wonder why he left his job.
（我在想他為什麼要辭職。）

I wonder who the girl is.
（我在想那女孩到底是誰。）

---

| act up<br>（機器）運轉<br>不正常 | The vacuum cleaner is acting up again.<br>（這吸塵器又出毛病了。） |
| | My car is acting up. I could hardly get it started this morning.<br>（我的車子又有毛病了。今天早上我幾乎沒辦法發動車子。） |

| ☑ beat | [bit] | 動 擊敗 |
|---|---|---|
| ☑ supposed | [sə'pozd] | （口語）應該 |
| ☑ copy machine | | 影印機 |
| ☑ electronics | [ɪlɛk'trɑnɪks] | 電子產品 |
| ☑ wonder | ['wʌndɚ] | 想知道 |
| ☑ vacuum cleaner | ['vækjʊəm 'klinɚ] | 吸塵器 |
| ☑ hardly | ['hɑrdlɪ] | 幾乎不 |

# 3 Be my guest.

請便

輕鬆學 有人到你家來作客，你是否都會對他客客氣氣的招
呼，所以，如果有人想跟你借用東西，而你也願意借
他的話，你可以跟他說 Be my guest. 這句話照字面
的意思是跟對方說「當我的客人」，既然讓他當你的
客人，也就是請他不用客氣，要借的東西儘管拿去
吧。

對話 一

A : My e-mail doesn't seem to be working today.

B : Mind if I have a look?

A : Be my guest.

> A：我的電子郵件今天不能用。
> B：我幫你看看你會介意嗎？
> A：請便。

18

## 對話 二

A : Can I borrow your sewing machine?

I'm making a Halloween costume for my son.

B : Be my guest, we never use it anyway.

A：我可以借你的縫紉機嗎？我在幫我兒子做萬聖節的服裝。

B：你儘管用，反正我們從不用。

## 加強練習

| mind<br>介意 | Do you mind if I smoke here?<br>（我在這裡抽煙，你介意嗎？） |  |
|---|---|---|
| | Do you mind if I sit here?<br>（我坐這裡，你介意嗎？） | |

**Can I ...?**
**我可以～？**

Can I borrow your car?

（我可以借你的車子嗎？）

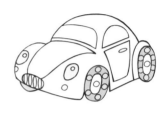

Can I open the window?

（我可以把窗戶打開嗎？）

  單　字

| ☑ mind | [maɪnd] | 動 介意 |
| ☑ guest | [gɛst] | 客人 |
| ☑ borrow | ['bɑro] | 動 借用 |
| ☑ sewing machine | | 縫紉機 |
| ☑ costume | ['kɑstjum] | 服裝 |

## 4 By the way

順便提一下

**輕鬆學** 不管你是有意提起，還是真的不經意的提起，在你跟別人的談話中，你突然想轉話題提問另一件事，你可以先說 By the way，再來說你想說的話，這樣一方面不會顯得太突兀，一方面也讓對方有個準備，知道你要提另一件事，不會一下子沒聽清楚你說的話。

**對話** 一

A： Here's Harry Potter.

I've finally finished it.

B： Thanks.

By the way, can you tell me which one of Harry's friends dies in the end?

I haven't had time to read it for myself.

A：這是哈利波特，你要看拿去。我終於看完了。

B：謝謝你，順便問一下，你可以告訴我到最後，哈力的哪一個朋友死掉嗎？我自己還沒時間看這本書。

## 對話 二

A : It's good to catch up with you again.

By the way, have you had a chance to look at that file I gave you yesterday?

B : Not yet, but I'll get right on it.

A：又再見到你了真好。

對了，你有機會看我昨天給你的檔案嗎？

B：還沒，但是我會馬上去看。

## 加 強 練 習

| Can you tell me...? 你可以告訴我 ... | Can you tell me where the library is? （你可以告訴我圖書館在哪裡嗎？） |
|---|---|
| | Can you tell me when the meeting is? （你可以告訴我會議是什麼時候嗎？） |

**I'll get right on it.**

我馬上去做

A : Please call John and ask him if he can pick up the children.

B : I'll get right on it.

A：請打電話給約翰，問他可以去接小孩子嗎？

B：我馬上去打。

 單  字

| ☑ finally | [ˈfaɪnl̩ɪ] | 最終；終於 |
| ☑ myself | [maɪˈsɛlf] | 我自己 |
| ☑ chance | [tʃæns] | 图 機會 |
| ☑ file | [faɪl] | 檔案 |

# 5 Can't beat that.

我不能做的更好

**輕鬆學** 前面說過 beat 這個字可以做「打敗」的意思，有人跟你吹噓說他做了一件多棒的事，或是用多便宜的價錢買到了某樣東西，你聽了，自認沒辦法「贏」過他所做的那件事，或是他所完成的交易，你只好回答他說 I can't beat that. 說這句話時，「I」可以省略掉，說 Can't beat that. 就好。

**對話 一**

A : I picked up this new computer including a complementary printer all for $500.

B : I can't beat that.

　　A：我買了這個電腦，包括贈送的印表機才美金五百元。

　　B：我不能用更好的價錢買到。

## 對話 二

A : I convinced John to sell me his 2000 Toyota Camry for $3000.

B : Wow! Can't beat that.

> A：我說服約翰賣我他的 2000 年的 Toyota Camry 賣三千元美金。.
>
> B：哇，我絕對買不到比那更好的價錢。

## 加強練習

---

| comple-mentary 贈送的 | McDonald's is offering complementary breakfasts to their first 50 customers tomorrow. |
|---|---|
| | 明天麥當勞要送他們的前五十個客人免費的早餐。 |
| | One day each year, May's Ice Cream gives out complementary ice cream cones to everyone. |
| | 每年，小美冰淇淋店都有一天免費贈送每人一客冰淇淋甜筒。 |

| convince<br>說服 | I convinced Mary to let me use her computer.<br>（我說服瑪麗讓我用她的電腦。） |
| | I have been trying to convince him to see a doctor.<br>（我一直在說服他去看醫生。） |

| ☑ computer | [kəm'pjutɚ] | 名 電腦 |
| ☑ include | [ɪn'klud] | 包括 |
| ☑ complementary | [ˌkɑmplə'mɛntərɪ] | 贈送的 |
| ☑ printer | ['prɪntɚ] | 印表機 |
| ☑ convince | [kən'vɪns] | 動 說服 |

# 6 Care to join us?

要跟我們一起來嗎？

**輕鬆學** care 是「喜歡」的意思，你們要去某個地方，邀約某個人一起去，問法就是 Do you care to join us? 這句話裡的 Do you 可以省略掉，就說 Care to join us?

**對話 一**

A : John, we're headed out to TGIF.
Care to join us?

B : No thanks, my wife is expecting me home
for dinner.

A：約翰，我們要去 TGIF。你要不要一起去？
B：不去，謝謝你們，我太太在等我回家吃晚飯。

對話 二

A : My husband and I have two extra tickets to the ballet tomorrow evening.

Care to join us?

B : That's sounds great. Let me check with my husband.

> A：我先生和我有多出兩張明晚的芭蕾舞的票。
>
> 要跟我們一起來嗎？
>
> B：聽起來是不錯。
>
> 我問我先生看看。

加 強 練 習

| | |
|---|---|
| **head**<br>前往 | We are headed to the beach.<br>（我們正要去海邊。）<br><br>Where are you headed?<br>（你們要去哪裡？） |

| expect<br>期待 | I am expecting an important phone call.<br>（我在等一通重要的電話。）<br><br>We are expecting company.<br>（我們在等客人。） |

單　字

| ☑ join | [dʒɔɪn] | 加入 |
|---|---|---|
| ☑ expect | [ɪkˋspɛkt] | 預期；期待 |
| ☑ extra | [ˋɛkstrə] | 額外的；多餘的 |
| ☑ ballet | [bæˋle] | 芭蕾舞 |
| ☑ ticket | [ˋtɪkɪt] | 票 |
| ☑ beach | [bitʃ] | 名 海濱 |
| ☑ important | [ɪmˋpɔrtənt] | 形 重要的 |
| ☑ company | [ˋkʌmpənɪ] | 名 朋友 |

# 7 Make yourself at home.

### 別拘束

輕鬆學 你在自己家裡的時候，是不是總覺得無拘無束，很自在，如果有人到你家來作客，你希望他能覺得很輕鬆自在，就跟他說 Make yourself at home. 他如果把你家當成跟他在自己家裡一樣，他就會覺得無拘無束了，輕鬆自在了。

## 對話 一

A : Hey!　Long time no see.
　　Come in and make yourself at home.
B : Thanks.　Let me just get the kids out of the car.

> A：嗨，好久不見。請進，別拘束。
> B：謝謝，我先到車子裡去帶小孩過來。

## 對話 二

A : Mrs. Lee.　Is it ok if I stay over for dinner?
B : Sure, come in and make yourself at home.

> A：李太太，我留下來吃晚飯可以嗎？
> B：當然可以，請進，別拘束。

加 強 練 習

| | |
|---|---|
| **kid**<br>小孩 | He is a smart kid.<br>（他是一個聰明的小孩。）<br><br>How many kids do you have?<br>（你有幾個小孩？） |
| **stay over**<br>留下來 | Are you going to stay over for dinner?<br>（你要留下來吃晚飯嗎？）<br><br>We have a spare bed if you want to stay over.<br>（如果你想留下來過夜，我們有多出一張床。） |

☑ kid      [kɪd]      小孩子

☑ yourself      [jʊrˈsɛlf]      你自己

☑ smart      [smɑrt]      聰明的

☑ spare      [spɛr]      形 多餘的

**Memo**

# 8 Could I get you something to drink?

MP3-9

你要喝什麼飲料嗎?

輕鬆學

有人到家裡來作客,中國人的傳統禮節是請對方喝茶,但是,現在社會可不一樣了,並不是每個人都喜歡喝茶,而且家家戶戶冰箱裡,可能都有各式的飲料,所以,有人到你家來作客,你不一定非要請他喝茶不可,尊重各人嗜好,問對方説 Could I get you something to drink? 這句話一方面提議要請對方喝飲料,一方面又讓對方選擇要什麼飲料。

對話 一

A : Mr. Smith should be finished with his meeting shortly.

Could I get you something to drink while we wait?

B : Water is fine.

> A:史密斯先生應該很快就會開完會。我們在等他的時候,你要我拿什麼飲料給你喝嗎?
>
> B:水就好。

**對話 二**

A : Welcome to TGIF.

Could I get you something to drink?

B : No thanks.

I'll wait for the rest of the party to arrive.

> A：歡迎到 TGIF 來。
>
> 你要喝什麼飲料嗎？
>
> B：不用了，謝謝你。
>
> 等其他人都到了之後再說。

**加 強 練 習**

| should 應該 | He should be here any time now.<br>（他應該隨時會到。） |
| --- | --- |
| | He should be in New York now.<br>（他現在應該是在紐約。） |

**Could I .....?**

我可以…嗎？

Could I get you any book to read?

（要我拿本書給你看嗎？）

Could I take your coat?

（要我把你的外套拿去掛起來嗎？）

| | | |
|---|---|---|
| ☑ drink | [drɪŋk] | 動 喝（飲料） |
| ☑ shortly | [ˈʃɔrtlɪ] | 一會兒 |
| ☑ finish | [ˈfɪnɪʃ] | 完成 |
| ☑ meeting | [ˈmitɪŋ] | 會議 |
| ☑ rest | [rɛst] | 其餘的 |

# 9 Could I have a lift?

能讓我搭個便車嗎？

**輕鬆學** lift 這個字大家可能學過是「把東西抬起來」的意思，這個字也可以做「搭便車」的意思，你如果想請朋友讓你搭便車，就問他 Could I have a lift?

## 對話 一

A : My car won't start. Could I have a lift?

B : No problem.

Hop in.

> A：我的車子沒法發動。能讓我搭個便車嗎？
> B：沒問題。進來吧。

## 對話 二

A : My father's working late today.

Could I have a lift home?

B : Sure. Get in.

> A：我父親今天會工作到晚一點。我可以搭你的便車回家嗎？
> B：當然可以，進來吧。

## 加 強 練 習

| | |
|---|---|
| **work**<br>工作 | Doctors often work very long hours.<br>（醫生工作的時間很長。）<br><br>Did you work overtime this week?<br>（這星期你有加班嗎？） |
| **start**<br>（車子）發動 | The car won't start.<br>（這部車沒辦法發動。）<br><br>I can't get the car started.<br>（我沒辦法讓這部車子發動。） |

單　　字

| ☑ lift | [lɪft] | （口語）搭便車 |
|---|---|---|
| ☑ hop | [hɑp] | 動 跳 |
| ☑ problem | [ˈprɑbləm] | 問題 |
| ☑ overtime | [ˈovɚˌtaɪm] | 加班 |

# 10 Cut it out.

別再這麼做

**輕鬆學** 有人每次遇到你，總喜歡開些你不喜歡的玩笑，一下子說你是不是昨晚沒睡好，要不然怎麼眼睛腫腫的，或是說你身上穿的那件衣服好土，他自認為很幽默，你卻生了一肚子悶氣，下次再遇到這種情形，別自己生悶氣了，跟他說 Cut it out. 叫他別再說這種無聊的玩笑。

## 對話 一

A : I don't appreciate being constantly teased.
Cut it out.

B : I'm sorry.
I didn't realize that it upset you so much.

> A：我不喜歡一直被嘲笑。別再這麼做了。
> B：對不起。我不知道那會令你那麼不高興。

## 對話 二

A : You know that I hate when you whistle in public.

Cut it out.

B : Okay, I'll try and remember.

> A：你知道嗎，我很討厭你在公共場合吹口哨。別再這麼做了。
> B：好的，我會盡量記得。

## 加強練習

**realize**
明瞭

I didn't realize she was upset.
（我不知道她不高興。）

I don't think you realize how important this is to me.
（我不認為你知道這對我有多重要。）

| **upset** 不高興 | Try not to let him upset you. （盡量不要為了他不高興。） |
| | It upset me when he talked on the phone all the time. （他總是在打電話，這件事令我很不高興。） |

 單  字

| ☑ appreciate | [əˈpriʃɪˌet] | **動** 感激 |
|---|---|---|
| ☑ constantly | [ˈkɑnstəntlɪ] | 不斷的；一再地 |
| ☑ tease | [tiz] | 嘲笑 |
| ☑ realize | [ˈriəˌlaɪz] | 明瞭；知道 |
| ☑ upset | [ˈʌpˈsɛt] | 不高興 |
| ☑ whistle | [ˈhwɪsl̩] | **動** 吹口哨 |
| ☑ public | [ˈpʌblɪk] | 公共的 |
| ☑ remember | [rɪˈmɛmbɚ] | 記得 |

# 11 Couldn't care less.

## 我才不在乎

**輕鬆學** care 是「在乎」的意思，Couldn't care less. 照字面的翻譯是「我不能在乎的更少」，意思是說，你已經是在乎的最少了，也就是說你一點都不在乎的意思，這句話完整的句子是 I couldn't care less. 說話時可以把「I」省略掉。

**對話**

A : Jack has the flu and can't come to school for a week.

B : What does that have to do with me?
I couldn't care less.

A：傑克得了流行性感冒，一個星期沒來上學。
B：那跟我有什麼關係。我才不在乎呢。

對話 二

A : My boss couldn't care less that he's given me too much to do.

B : That's life.

Get used to it.

A：我老闆才不在乎他會給我太多的工作。

B：人生就是這樣。習慣了就好。

加 強 練 習

| flu<br>流行性感冒 | She's been in bed with the flu.<br>（她患流行性感冒，一直在床。） |
| | I think I'm coming down with the flu.<br>（我想我可能患了流行性感冒。） |

| get used to 習慣;適應 | Don't worry. You'll soon get used to the cold.<br>（別擔心,你很快就會適應這種冷。）<br>――――――――――――――<br>I could never get used to living in a big city.<br>（我永遠沒辦法適應大<br>都市的生活。）  |
|---|---|

| ☑ flu | [flu] | 流行性感冒 |
|---|---|---|
| ☑ care | [kɛr] | 關心;在乎;在意 |
| ☑ less | [lɛs] | 較少的 |
| ☑ boss | [bɔs] | 名 主管;老闆 |
| ☑ city | [ˈsɪtɪ] | 都市 |

# 12 Don't ask.

你就別問了。

**輕鬆學** 你遇到不順心的事情，有時你也想跟朋友說一說，以便抒解一下情緒，但是，有時事情實在太複雜，一時也說不清楚，有些事情，你則是不想再提，這時若是有朋友關心的問你，出了什麼事嗎？你既然不想講，或是講不清楚，你就可以跟他說 Don't ask.

**對話** 一

A : You look terrible today.
    What's happened?

B : Long story, don't ask.

> A ：你今天看起來很狼狽。發生了什麼事？
> B ：說來話長，你就別問了。

## 對話 二

A： Ever since Tom came back from meeting with his boss he's been very angry.

I wonder what happened.

B： Don't ask.

Some things are better left alone.

> A：湯姆跟他的老闆開了會回來之後，就一直很生氣。
> 我真想知道發生了什麼事。
> B：你就別問了。有些事別管較好。

## 加 強 練 習

| terrible | What terrible news! |
| --- | --- |
| 糟透的； | （真是糟透了的消息！） |
| 不高興；生病 |  |
| | You look terrible; you'd better sit down. |
| | （你看起來不妙，你最好坐下。） |

## leave
剩下；留下

Is there any juice left?

（還有沒有果汁剩下？）

You'd better leave him alone.

（你最好別理他。）

 單  字

☑ terrible [ˈtɛrəbl̩] （口語）糟透的

☑ happen [ˈhæpən] 發生

☑ back [bæk] 回來

☑ angry [ˈæŋgrɪ] 生氣的

☑ alone [əˈlon] 形 單獨的；獨自

# 13 Don't bother.

### 別麻煩

**輕鬆學** 你到別人家作客，主人殷勤的招呼你，一下子要倒茶水，又要問你需要什麼嗎，你不想太打擾主人，趕緊跟他說，Don't bother. 大家坐下來聊聊天就好。

你去約翰家要找約翰，他的家人告訴你他在睡覺，而要去叫醒他，你只是過來坐坐，沒什麼大不了的事，不想因此去吵醒約翰，那就趕緊跟他的家人說 Don't bother.

**對話 一**

A : Let me get you some lemonade.

B : Don't bother.  I won't be staying long.

> A：我去拿一些檸檬汁給你。
> B：別麻煩，我不會待太久。

## 對話 二

A： Jack's upstairs sleeping.

　　Do you want me to wake him up?

B： Don't bother. It's not that important.

> A：傑克在樓上睡覺。
>
> 　　你要我去叫醒他嗎？
>
> B：別麻煩，我沒什麼重要的事。

## 加 強 練 習

| wake someone up 把某人叫醒 | A cold shower will soon wake you up. （洗個冷水澡，會讓你清醒。） |
| --- | --- |
| | Try not to wake the baby up. （盡量不要把嬰孩吵醒。） |

**awake**

醒著

A : John, are you awake?

B : I am now, but I was asleep.

A：約翰，你醒著嗎？

B：我現在醒了，但是，剛剛我在睡覺。

單　　字

| ☑ lemonade | [ˌlɛmənˈed] | 檸檬汁 |
| ☑ bother | [ˈbɑðɚ] | 動 麻煩 |
| ☑ upstairs | [ʌpˈstɛrz] | 樓上 |
| ☑ shower | [ʃaʊr] | 淋浴 |
| ☑ awake | [əˈwek] | 醒著 |

# 14 Don't speak too soon.

## 話不要說的太快

**輕鬆學** 世事往往很難料，如果有人嘴巴大，喜歡鐵口直斷的說這件事、那件事將如何，你可以跟他說 Don't speak too soon. 話講的那麼快，沒什麼好處的。

**對話** 一

A： If the bull market continues, I stand to make a fortune in a few years.

B： The stock market is very unpredictable. Don't speak too soon.

> A：如果股票市場持續往上飆，我幾年內就會賺翻了。
> B：股票市場很難預測的。話不要說的太快。

## 對話 (二)

A： Looks like John and Mary are fighting again. They just might get a divorce this time around.

B： Don't speak too soon. Those two are very good at reconciling.

> A：看起來約翰和瑪麗又在吵架了。他們很快就會離婚的。
>
> B：話不要說的太快。他們兩個一下子又和好了。

## 加強練習

| make a fortune 賺了一筆 | He made a fortune in the stock. （他在股票上賺了一筆。） |
|---|---|
| | He invested in real estate and hoped to make a fortune in it. （他投資在房地產，希望能在那上面賺一筆。） |

**market**
市場

I don't think the bull market would continue long.

（我不認為股市牛市會持續很久。）

People can make money in either a bull market or a bear market.

（不管股市是牛市，還是熊市，人們都能賺到錢。）

**Memo**

| | | |
|---|---|---|
| ☑ market | ['mɑrkɪt] | 市場 |
| ☑ continue | [kən'tɪnju] | 勳 繼續 |
| ☑ fortune | ['fɔrtʃən] | 財富 |
| ☑ unpredictable | [ʌn'prɪdɪktəb!] | 不可預測的 |
| ☑ stock | [stɑk] | 股票 |
| ☑ divorce | [dɪ'vɔrs] | 離婚 |
| ☑ reconcile | ['rɛkən‚saɪl] | 和解；和好 |
| ☑ invest | [ɪn'vɛst] | 投資 |

# 15 Don't work too hard.

### 別工作的太勞累

輕鬆學　有人剛病後回來上班，你可以關心的提醒他說 Don't work too hard. 這句話用在這裡是真的在關心他別工作的太勞累。有時候，下班時間到，你要下班了，公司裡還有同事繼續在工作著，你除了跟他們說再見之外，還可以加一句 Don't work too hard. 這時候，這句話只是你要下班之前跟同事說的一句俏皮話而已。

對話 一

A : You've only just recovered from your heart attack.

Don't work too hard.

B : Don't worry.

　　A：你的心臟病剛好。別工作得太勞累。

　　B：別擔心。

## 對話 二

A : Aren't we going out later this evening?

B : Yes, so don't work too hard today.
Leave some energy for tonight.

A：我們稍晚不是要出去嗎？
B：是的，所以別工作的太勞累。留些精力今晚用。

## 加強練習

| | |
|---|---|
| **recover** <br> 恢復 | He's still recovering from a heart attack. <br> （他還在從心臟病恢復當中。） |
| | After a few days of having a cold, he began to recover. <br> （幾天感冒之後，他現在開始恢復。） |

| Aren't we...?<br>我們不是…？ | Aren't we going to the movies this Friday?<br>（我們這星期五不是要去看電影嗎？） |
| --- | --- |
| | Aren't we having a long weekend soon?<br>（我們不是很快就會有長週末嗎？） |

單　　字

| ☑ recover | [rɪˈkʌvɚ] | 恢復 |
| --- | --- | --- |
| ☑ heart attack | | 心臟病 |
| ☑ energy | [ˈɛnɚdʒɪ] | 活力 |
| ☑ cold | [kold] | 名 感冒 |
| ☑ weekend | [ˈwikˈɛnd] | 名 週末 |
| ☑ soon | [sun] | 很快地 |

# 16 Drop it!

**別再說了**

輕鬆學 剛剛說過，你遇到不順心的事，又不想跟別人說，偏偏有人問起時，你就可以跟他說 Don't ask. 這種情形除了說這句話之話，也可以說 Drop it!，這句話裡 drop 是「丟掉」的意思，it 指對方問的問題，叫對方把他問的問題丟掉，就是叫他不要提這個問題。

## 對話 一

A： What were you and Mary arguing about back there?

B： It's none of your business. Drop it.

> A：你跟瑪麗在後面爭吵什麼？
> B：沒你的事。你就別提了。

## 對話 二

A : Drop it already!

I'm tired of you badgering me.

B : Don't get angry with me.

I'm only trying to help.

> A：不要再說了。
>
> 我對你問個不停很煩了。
>
> B：別生我的氣。
>
> 我只是想幫你的忙。

## 加強練習

| | |
|---|---|
| **None of your business.** 沒你的事 | A : How much is the diamond ring you are wearing? B : None of your business. |

A：你戴的鑽戒多少錢？

B：沒你的事。

| I'm only trying to... 我只是想… | I'm only trying to find out the truth. （我只是想找出真相。） |
| :--- | :--- |
| | Don't be mad at him. He's only trying to help. （別生他的氣，他只是想幫忙。） |

| ☑ argue | [ˈɑrgjʊ] | 動 爭辯 |
| :--- | :--- | :--- |
| ☑ badger | [ˈbædʒɚ] | 糾纏；困擾 |
| ☑ diamond | [ˈdaɪəmənd] | 鑽石 |
| ☑ ring | [rɪŋ] | 戒指 |
| ☑ wear | [wɛr] | 動 穿；戴 |
| ☑ truth | [truθ] | 事實 |

# 17 Excuse me.

### 對不起

**輕鬆學** 當你想請前面的人讓路,你好過去時,要說 Excuse me. 你說了這句話,只要懂得英語的人都會知道你是在請他讓路,至於讓不讓,那就要看對方囉。

在人潮擁擠的地方,你不小心撞倒別人,或是踩到別人的腳,要趕緊跟對方說 Excuse me. 這句話在這裡是真的在跟對方「道歉」的意思。

**對話**

A : Excuse me.  Please let me through.

I'm in a hurry.

B : Wait your turn.

You're not the only person in a rush.

> A:對不起,請讓我過去。我有急事。
> B:等輪到你吧。你又不是第一個有急事的。

對話 (二)

A： Excuse me.

Sorry for bumping into you.

B： It's ok. It's very crowded in here.

> A：對不起。不好意思撞上你了。
>
> B：沒關係，這裡很擁擠。

加 強 練 習

| **rush**<br>匆忙；趕 | What's the rush? I'm almost done.<br>（趕什麼？我快好了。） |
| | We don't need to rush.  We have plenty of time.<br>（我們不用趕，我們有很多時間。） |

| bump into 撞上；不期而遇 | It was so dark. She bumped into a tree.<br>（天色很暗，她一不小心撞上了一棵樹。）<br><br>I bumped into John this morning.<br>（我今天早上與約翰不期而遇。） |

| ☑ through | [θru] | 穿越 |
|---|---|---|
| ☑ hurry | [ˈhɝɪ] | 匆忙；趕快 |
| ☑ turn | [tɝn] | 輪流 |
| ☑ rush | [rʌʃ] | 緊急的；急著趕 |
| ☑ bump | [bʌmp] | 撞到 |
| ☑ crowded | [ˈkraʊdɪd] | 形 擁擠的 |
| ☑ dark | [dɑrk] | 形 天黑的 |

# 18 Forget it!

免談

輕鬆學 有人跟你借東西,常喜歡玩「借荊州霸荊州」的遊戲,借給他的東西,肯定是有去無回,今天他又來跟你借上課抄的筆記,趕緊斬釘斷鐵的跟他說 Forget it! 讓他不要再跟你糾纏個沒完。

### 對話 一

A : Forget it.

I'm not letting you borrow my notes again.

You never returned them last time.

B : Please give me another chance.

I promise to return them this time.

> A:免談。我不可能再把筆記簿借給你。上一次你根本沒有還我。
>
> B:請再給我一次機會。我保證這次一定還你。

### 對話 二

A ： Can I ask a favor from you?

B ： Forget it!

This is the third one this week.

A：我可以請你幫個忙嗎？

B：免談。

這已是這個星期第三次了。

### 加強練習

| **I'm not letting you....** 我不會讓你… | I'm not letting you borrow my car again. （我不會再讓你借我的車子。） |
|---|---|
| | I'm not letting you use my computer again. （我不會再讓你用我的電腦。） |

**I promise....**
我答應；我保證

I promise to pay you back this time.
（我保證這次一定會還你錢。）

I promised to take care of her plants while she is away.
（我答應在她不在的時候，替她照顧花草。）

**Memo**

## 單　字

| | | | |
|---|---|---|---|
| ☑ borrow | [ˈbɑro] | **動** | 借用 |
| ☑ note | [not] | **名** | 筆記 |
| ☑ return | [rɪˈtɝn] | | 歸還 |
| ☑ another | [əˈnʌðɚ] | | 另一個 |
| ☑ chance | [tʃæns] | **名** | 機會 |
| ☑ promise | [ˈprɑmɪs] | | 承諾；保證；答應 |
| ☑ favor | [ˈfevɚ] | | （美語）幫忙；恩惠 |
| ☑ forget | [fɚˈgɛt] | | 忘記 |
| ☑ plant | [plænt] | **名** | 植物 |

## 19 Get lost!

MP3-20

走開

輕鬆學 Get lost! 這句話大家一定學過是「迷了路」的意思，來看看這個情形，一個男孩子喜歡一個女孩子，老是在她身邊繞個不停，纏著要約她去看電影，要請她吃飯，女孩子實在煩透了，就跟他說 Get lost!，奇怪了可沒有人迷路了啊，注意，女孩說這句話的意思是叫這個男孩在她的面前消失掉，不要在她的面前再出現。

對話 一

A : Get lost!

I really don't want to see you right now.

B : Don't be blaming me for your mistakes.

It's not my fault you got into trouble with your boss.

> A：走開。我現在不想看到你。
>
> B：別把你的錯誤怪到我頭上來。你跟你的老闆有麻煩，不是我的錯。

## 對話 二

A：Get lost!

Haven't you caused enough trouble here already?

B：I'm sorry.

I only came back to see how I could help.

> A：走開。你在這裡惹的禍還不夠多嗎？
>
> B：對不起。我只是回來看看我能幫得上什麼忙嗎？

## 加強練習

| It's not my fault... 那不是我的錯 | It's not my fault you were late for school.<br>（你上學遲到又不是我的錯。） |
|---|---|
| | It's all your fault I missed the bus again.<br>（我又沒搭上公車都是你的錯。） |

| blame | If anyone's to blame, it's me. |
| 怪罪 | （如果要怪，就怪我。） |
| | Don't blame me if you fail the exam. |
| | （如果你考試考不及格，不要怪我。） |

單　　字

| ☑ really | ['rɪəlɪ] | 真的 |
| ☑ blame | [blem] | 歸罪於 |
| ☑ mistake | [mə'stek] | 名 錯誤 |
| ☑ fault | [fɔlt] | 過錯 |
| ☑ trouble | ['trʌbl̩] | 麻煩；困難 |
| ☑ cause | [kɔz] | 動 引起 |

# 20 Get off my back!

## 別繼續煩我

**輕鬆學** 有人爬在你的背上，你說煩不煩，如果有人一天到晚纏著你，要你做這做那，叨叨不停的叮嚀你，即使對方是好意，也可能跟有人爬在你背上一樣的煩，要叫對方不要煩你，英語有句話就是 Get off my back! 夠傳神吧。

## 對話 一

A : John, have you finished working on that file I gave you?

B : Get off my back already!

I've got a lot to do this week.

> A：約翰，我給你的檔案你做完了嗎？
>
> B：別來吵我。我這星期要做的事情很多。

## 對話 二

A： I'm tired of my mother always nagging me about cleaning my room.

I wish she would get off my back already.

B： Well, that's the way parents are.

> A：我對我媽媽一直嘮叨著要我整理我的房間，真的很煩。我真希望她不要再來煩我。
>
> B：做父母的，就是那樣。

## 加強練習

| | |
|---|---|
| **finish**<br>完成 | Have you finished reading the newspaper?<br>（你報紙看完了嗎？） |
| | Have you finished washing the dishes?<br>（你碗碟洗完了嗎？） |

**nag**
嘮叨

Stop nagging. I'll do it as soon as I get time.

（不要再嘮叨了。我一有時間就會做。）

She's been nagging him to clean the room.

（她一直在嘮叨著要他去整理房間。）

| ☑ back | [bæk] | 名 背部 |
| --- | --- | --- |
| ☑ file | [faɪl] | 檔案 |
| ☑ nag | [næg] | 嘮叨 |
| ☑ finish | [ˈfɪnɪʃ] | 完成 |

# 21 Give me a call.

## 給我打個電話

**輕鬆學** 男女朋友相聚了一天,該分手各自回家去了,可又依依不捨的,不禁又叮嚀了一句,回到家,Give me a call.。這句話可不一定是依依不捨時叮嚀用的,大家有正事要談,你也可以叮嚀對方,記得 Give me a call.

**對話 一**

A : Give me a call when you get home.

B : Sure thing.

> A:你回到家給我打個電話。
>
> B:好的。

## 對話 二

A： I'm going to be in a meeting most of the afternoon.

I'll give you a call when I get out.

B： Sounds good.

Maybe we can go get some dinner afterwards.

> A：今天下午我大部分的時間在開會。我開完會就會打個電話給你。
>
> B：好的。或許之後我們就可以去吃晚飯。

## 加強練習

| I'll ...<br>我會 | I'll give you a call when I get there.<br>（我一到那裡就會給你打電話。） |
| --- | --- |
| | I'll let you know when I hear from him.<br>（我一有他的消息就會讓你知道。） |

| **I'm going to...**<br>我要 | I'm going to play tennis with Mary on Friday.<br>（我星期五要跟瑪麗打網球。） |
| | I'm going to see a doctor soon.<br>（我很快會去看醫生。） |

| ☑ most | [most] | 大多數 |
| ☑ sound | [saʊnd] | **動** 聽起來 |
| ☑ afterwards | [ˈæftɚwɚdz] | 其後；之後 |
| ☑ tennis | [tɛnɪs] | 網球 |

# 22 Good luck!

祝你好運。

輕鬆學　你明知對方有麻煩，例如：他把新車給撞壞了，回家一定挨罵，你沒有別的話可以安慰他，只好跟他說 Good luck! 了，除了寄望 luck（幸運），希望事情不要太糟又能怎麼辦呢。對方有一個重要的考試，或是要去面談工作，這些都不是你能幫得上忙的，也只好跟他說 Good luck! 了。

對話 一

A : I'm going to go tell my parents that I wrecked my new car.

B : Good luck!

A：我要去跟我的父母說，我把我的新車撞毀了。
B：祝你好運。

**對話 二**

A : I have a very important exam coming up in a few days.

B : Good luck!

I know you will do well.

A：過幾天我有一個很重要的考試。

B：祝你好運。我知道你一定可以考得很好。

**加 強 練 習**

| wreck<br>車子撞毀；車禍 | My son wrecked the car yesterday.<br>（我兒子昨天把車子撞毀了。）<br>There is a really bad wreck on the highway right now.<br>（高速公路上現在有一個很嚴重的車禍。） |

| **I am going to ...**<br>我將要… | I am going to wash the car this weekend.<br>（我這個週末要洗車子。）<br><br>I am going to visit my grandparents tomorrow.<br>（我明天要去看我的祖父母。） |

單　　字

| ☑ wreck | [rɛk] | （口語）撞車 |
| ☑ luck | [lʌk] | 運氣 |
| ☑ really | ['riəlɪ] | 真的 |
| ☑ highway | ['haɪwe] | 公路；高速公路 |

MP3-24

# 23 Guess what!

## 你猜猜看什麼事

輕鬆學 ▶ 有人在跟別人說一件他覺得很興奮的事情，或是他自認很新鮮的新聞時，喜歡先說句 Guess what!，一副神秘兮兮要人家猜他要說什麼的樣子，注意，通常有人跟你說 Guess what! 時，並不是真的要讓你猜他要說什麼，這只是一種說話的習慣而已，有時他在說完 Guess what! 之後，會繼續說他要說的話，你也可以在他跟你說 Guess what! 時，回一句 What? 對方就會繼續把要說的新聞說出來。

## 對話 一

A : Guess what!

My mom just gave birth to a new baby sister.

B : That's terrific news.

What's her name?

> A：猜猜看是什麼事。我母親剛給我生了一個新妹妹。
> B：那真是好消息。她叫什麼名字？

## 對話 （二）

A： Guess what!

Mark is coming back from Iraq next week.

He's finally getting a few weeks of leave.

B： I know you must be excited that he's coming home.

> A：你猜猜看什麼事。
>
> 馬克下星期將從伊拉克回來。
>
> 他終於有了幾個星期的假。
>
> B：我知道你一定很興奮他要回家來。

## 加 強 練 習

| give birth to 生 | She gave birth to a new boy last week. （她上個星期生了一個男孩。） |
|---|---|
| | Mary gave birth to her first child yesterday. （瑪麗昨天生了頭胎。） |

| leave<br>請假 | I'm going to take three days' leave.<br>（我要請三天假。）<br><br>Who's going to be in charge when John's on leave?<br>（約翰請假時，要由誰負責？） |
| --- | --- |

單　字

| ☑ terrific | [təˈrɪfɪk] | 很好的 |
| --- | --- | --- |
| ☑ news | [njuz] | 新聞 |
| ☑ finally | [ˈfaɪnḷɪ] | 最終；終於 |
| ☑ excited | [ɪkˈsaɪtɪd] | 感到興奮的 |
| ☑ leave | [liv] | 請假 |

# 24 Have a good day.

祝你一天愉快

**輕鬆學** Have a good day. 這句話是兩個人說再見時，多加的一句祝福的話，希望對方一整天都很愉快，有人跟你說這句話，你可以回答 Thank you.，你也可以回答 You too. 說這句話就是，你也祝福對方一天愉快的意思。

### 對話 一

A： I'm going home now. Have a good day.

B： Thanks. I think I'm going to be here a while.

　　A：我要回家了。祝你一天愉快。

　　B：謝謝你。我想我還要在這裡多待一會兒。

### 對話 二

A： Ok, I'm off to my first class of the day.

B： Have a good day!

　　A：好了，我要去上我的第一天課了。

　　B：祝你一天愉快。

加 強 練 習

| | |
|---|---|
| **off**<br>離開 | I must be off soon.<br>（我很快就得走了。）<br><br>Good bye. I'm off to work now.<br>（再見，我要去上班了。） |
| **I'm going<br>to ...**<br>我將要… | I'm going to take a vacation next<br>week.<br>（我下星期要去度假。）<br><br>I'm going to visit Mary tonight.<br>（我今晚要去拜訪瑪麗。） |

| | | |
|---|---|---|
| ☑ while | [hwaɪl] | 一段時間 |
| ☑ first | [fɝst] | 第一 |
| ☑ vacation | [vəˈkeʃən] | 图 休假；假期 |

# 25 Have fun.

祝你玩得愉快

**輕鬆學** 跟對方説 Have a good day. 是一句可以隨時掛在嘴上説的話，但是，如果對方是要去玩，或是去休息消遣一類的，那就跟他説 Have fun. 吧，因為他要去做的事就是要去 fun 的，所以你就祝他 have fun 吧。

**對話 一**

A : I think I'm going to put off finishing my science project this weekend and go to the beach instead.

B : Have fun.

> A：我想我這個週末還不想把科學研究作業做完，我要到海邊去。
>
> B：祝你玩得愉快。

## 對話 ㈡

A： My wife is going shopping with some girlfriends.

I'm going to be taking care of the kids today.

B： Try to have fun.

Kids can be a handful.

A：我太太要跟她的幾個女朋友去逛街。今天我要照顧小孩。

B：盡量保持愉快。小孩子有時很累人的。

## 加強練習

| instead<br>相反的 | I'm not going to the party. I'm going to read a book at home instead.<br>（我不要去參加宴會，相反的，我要留在家裡看書。） |
| --- | --- |
| | I'm not going to cook tonight.  I'm taking my family out for dinner instead.<br>（我今晚不煮飯，相反的，我要帶家人去吃晚飯。） |

| put off 延期 | We'll have to put off going on vacation until we get time. （我們的假期要延期，直到我們有時間。） |

You can't just keep putting it off.
（你不能一直延期。）

| ☐ put off | | 延期 |
| ☐ science | ['saɪəns] | 科學 |
| ☐ project | ['prɑdʒɛkt] | 專案；企畫；學校研究作業 |
| ☐ instead | [ɪn'stɛd] | 不是 … 而是 … |
| ☐ handful | ['hæd,fʊl] | 麻煩事 |

# 26 **Help yourself.**

你儘管拿

輕鬆學 東西如果是需要人家拿給你的話,第一,要看人家要
給你多少,第二,你如果要多一點,可能也會不好意
思,如果自己拿,別人沒看見的話,那可好,要拿多
少就拿多少,所以,你如果想要什麼東西,對方叫你
Help yourself. 那就是叫你自己儘管拿的意思。

## 對話 一

A : Mind if I grab a piece of fruit from the
table?

I haven't eaten all day.

B : Help yourself.

> A:我在桌上拿個水果吃,你不介意吧?我一整天都
> 沒吃東西。
>
> B:你儘管拿。

## 對話 二

A : You have quite a few good rock albums.
Can I take a few home to listen to?

B : Sure, help yourself.

A：你有不少好的搖滾唱片。我可以拿幾張回去聽嗎？

B：沒問題，你儘管拿。

## 加 強 練 習

| mind<br>介意 | Do you mind if I smoke here?<br>（我在這裡抽煙，你介意嗎？） |
|---|---|
| | Do you mind driving? I'm not feeling well.<br>（你開車好嗎？我覺得不太舒服。） |

**I haven't ...**
我沒有…

I haven't eaten all day.
（我一整天都沒有吃東西。）

I haven't heard from him yet.
（我還沒聽到他的消息。）

單　　字

| ☑ mind | [maɪnd] | 動介意 |
| ☑ grab | [græb] | 匆忙地拿；隨便吃一下 |
| ☑ rock | [rɑk] | 搖滾樂 |
| ☑ album | [ˈælbəm] | 唱片 |

# 27 Hurry up!

快一點

**輕鬆學** 你眼看著就快趕不上火車或是飛機,或者你們要去看表演的時間就快到了,某人還在拖拖拉拉,拉開嗓門叫他 Hurry up! 吧。

**對話** 一

A : Hurry up, Megan!
    We're going to be late for church.
B : I'm coming.
    Sorry for making everyone wait for me.

> A:快一點,梅根。我們上教堂要遲到了。
> B:我來了。對不起,讓大家都在等我。

**對話** 二

A : The show starts in 20 minutes.
    Will you please hurry up?
B : Just give me a few more minutes.
    I'll be right down.

> A:表演再二十分就要開始。你快一點行嗎?
> B:再給我幾分鐘。我馬上下來。

## 加 強 練 習

| | |
|---|---|
| **We're going to ....** 我們將會… | We're going to be late for school.<br>（我們上學將會遲到。）<br><br>We're going to miss the bus.<br>（我們將會搭不上公車。） |
| **start** 開始 | When does the school start?<br>（什麼時候開學？）<br><br>The show starts at 7:30.<br>（表演七點半開始。） |

單　字

| ☑ late | [let] | 遲到 |
|---|---|---|
| ☑ wait | [wet] | 等 |
| ☑ show | [ʃo] | 表演；節目 |
| ☑ miss | [mɪs] | 動 錯過 |

# 28 I can't help it.

**我沒辦法啊。**

輕鬆學 人生在世，不如意事十常八九，有些事還真不是你能
掌控的，遇到這樣的事，如果有人跟你抱怨的話，你
只好跟他説 I can't help it. 我沒辦法啊。

## 對話 一

A : Why are you always late for work?

B : I can't help it.

My car has been giving me a lot of
problems.

> A：你上班為什麼總是遲到？
>
> B：我沒辦法啊。我的車子總是給我很多麻煩。

## 對話 二

A : Your voice is annoyingly high pitched.

B : I can't help it.

I was born with it.

> A：你的聲音很高昂，聽起來很煩。
>
> B：我沒辦法。我生來就是這樣。

加 強 練 習

| | |
|---|---|
| **be late for**<br>遲到 | John is always late for work.<br>（約翰上班總是遲到。）<br><br>Is John late for work again?<br>（約翰上班又遲到了嗎？） |
| **problem**<br>問題 | Let me know if you have any problems.<br>（如果你有任何問題，讓我知道。）<br><br>I have a serious problem, and I don't know what to do.<br>（我有一個很嚴重的問題，我不知道該怎麼辦。） |

| | | |
|---|---|---|
| ☑ always | [ˈɔlwez] | 總是 |
| ☑ problem | [ˈprɑbləm] | 問題 |
| ☑ annoyingly | [əˈnɔɪŋlɪ] | 惱人的 |
| ☑ pitched | [ˈpɪtʃɪd] | 高音的 |
| ☑ voice | [vɔɪs] | 名 聲音 |
| ☑ serious | [ˈsɪrɪəs] | 嚴重的 |

**Memo**

# 29 I can't say for sure.

## 我不太確定

輕鬆學 有些事你也沒有肯定的答案,因為你自己也不太確定,遇到這樣的事,你就跟對方説 I can't say for sure.

### 對話 一

A : What time did you finally get to sleep last night?

B : I can't say for sure.
I fell asleep at my desk.

> A:你昨晚幾點去睡?
> B:我說不上來。我在桌子上睡著了。

### 對話 二

A : Who do you think will win the track meet today?

B : I can't say for sure.
There are several strong competitors.

> A:你認為今天的田徑賽誰會贏?
> B:這我不能確定。今天的比賽選手有幾個蠻強的。

## 加 強 練 習

| | |
|---|---|
| **What time...?**<br>什麼時候 | What time did you get up this morning?<br>（你今早幾點起床？）<br><br>What time did you call Mary?<br>（你什麼時候打電話給瑪麗？） |
| **fall asleep**<br>睡著 | John fell asleep in class yesterday.<br>（約翰昨天在課堂上睡著。） |

Mary fell asleep at her desk again.
（瑪麗又在桌上睡著了。）

| ☐ finally | [ˈfaɪnḷɪ] | 最終；終於 |
| ☐ asleep | [əˈslip] | 形 睡著的 |
| ☐ track meet | | 田徑賽 |
| ☐ several | [ˈsɛvrəl] | 幾個 |
| ☐ competitor | [kəmˈpɪtɪtɚ] | 競爭者 |

**Memo**

# 30 I can't thank you enough.

### 我真不知道該怎麼感謝你

**輕鬆學** 如果有人幫了你一個大忙，你要跟他説幾聲謝謝才
夠呢，有些忙是讓你感激到不管説多少聲謝謝都不
夠的，那就跟他説 I can't thank you enough. 吧。
enough 是「足夠」的意思，説再多的謝謝也不夠，
就説這麼一句話就把所有的謝意都表達清楚了。

## 對話 一

A : I can't thank you enough for helping me out.

B : Don't worry about it.

　　Glad to be of service.

　　　　A：你幫我的忙，我真不知道要怎麼感謝你。

　　　　B：沒什麼。

　　　　　　我很高興幫得上忙。

對話 二

A : I spoke with my boss about job openings in our company.

I think he's agreed to interview you.

B : I can't thank you enough for getting me this opportunity.

A：關於我們公司有的職位空缺，我跟我老闆說了。

我想他答應跟你面談。

B：你給了我這個機會，我真不知道要怎麼感謝你。

加強練習

| service<br>服務 | Can I be of service to anyone?<br>（有人需要我的服務嗎？）<br><br>The service here is terrible.<br>（這裡的服務真差。） |

| job openings 職位空缺 | Do you have any job openings in your company?<br>（你們公司有什麼職位空缺嗎？）<br><br>Our company has some job openings.<br>（我們公司有一些職位空缺。） |
| --- | --- |

單　　字

☑ service　　['sɝvɪs]　　服務

☑ spoke　　[spok]　　說

☑ opening　　['opənɪŋ]　　職缺

☑ company　　['kʌmpənɪ]　　公司

☑ agree　　[ə'gri]　　動 同意

☑ interview　　['ɪntɚvju]　　名 面談

☑ terrible　　['tɛrəbl]　　差勁的；（口語）糟透的

# 31 I'd better be going.

我得走了。

輕鬆學 had better 是「最好」的意思，天晚了，你覺得你該走了，你還有其他事情要做，你覺得你該走了，或是時間到了，你該走了，英語的說法就是 I'd better be going.

 對話 一

A : It's getting late. I'd better be going.

B : Ok. I see you tomorrow then.

> A：很晚了。我得走了。
> B：好，明天見。

對話 二

A : My wife is expecting me home for dinner, so I'd better be going.

B : She's lucky to have a husband who's so conscious of not being late.

> A：我太太在家等我吃晚飯，所以我得走了。
> B：她真幸運，有這麼個丈夫很注意不要遲到。

## 加 強 練 習

| | |
|---|---|
| **It's getting....**<br>天漸漸地… | It's getting light.<br>（天漸漸亮了。） |
| | It's getting dark.<br>（天漸漸暗了。） |

| | |
|---|---|
| **expect**<br>期待 | We are expecting company.<br>（我們在等客人。） |
| | She is expecting John to call her.<br>（她在等著約翰打電話給她。） |

單 字

| | | |
|---|---|---|
| ☐ conscious | [ˈkɑnʃəs] | 意識到的 |
| ☐ light | [laɪt] | 形 光亮的 |
| ☐ dark | [dɑrk] | 形 天黑的 |

# 32 I didn't catch your name.

## 我沒聽清楚你的名字。

輕鬆學 有些人你見過面，但是不管對方是告訴過你他的名字，還是沒有，總之，你只知道你見過那個人，卻不知道他叫什麼名字，你就可以跟他說，I didn't catch your name. 對方如果願意告訴你他叫什麼名字，他就會跟你說。

對話 一

A : Hi!

We met yesterday at the press conference, but I didn't catch your name.

B : Yes, I remember you.

My name is Jenny Lee.

> A：嗨。我們昨天在記者會上見過面，但是我沒聽清楚你的名字。
>
> B：是的，我記得你。我的名字是李珍妮。

### 對話 二

A： You look very familiar.

I think you are in my math class.

B： I recognize you, too.

I didn't catch your name though.

> A：你看起來很面熟。
>
> 我想你跟我一起上數學課。
>
> B：我也認出你了。
>
> 但是我不知道你的名字。

### 加 強 練 習

| remember<br>記得 | Did you remember to bring my book for me?<br>（你有沒有記得把我的書拿來給我？） |
| --- | --- |
| | I didn't remember I told her the story.<br>（我不記得我有跟她說那個故事。） |

| familiar<br>熟悉 | You look familiar.<br>（你看起來很熟悉。） |
| | He looks familiar to me, but I can't place him.<br>（我覺得他很面熟，但是我想不起他是誰。） |

單　　字

| ☑ catch | [kætʃ] | 跟上並理解 |
| ☑ press | [prɛs] | 名 報章雜誌 |
| ☑ conference | [ˈkɑnfərəns] | 會議；研討會 |
| ☑ familiar | [fəˈmɪljɚ] | 熟悉 |
| ☑ recognize | [ˈrɛkəgˌnaɪz] | 認得；認出 |
| ☑ though | [ðo] | （口語）不過 |

# 33 I didn't get that.

我沒弄清楚

輕鬆學 ger 這個字可以做「聽懂別人意思」，有人說的話，你沒有聽懂，你就可以跟他說 I didn't get that. 請他再說清楚。若是有人說笑話，You didn't get that. 那就不是對方再重說一次，你就可以 get that. 最好請他把他說的笑話解釋一下吧。

對話 一

A : Can you repeat what you just said?
    I didn't get that.
B : You should pay closer attention then.

> A：請你把剛剛說過的，再說一次好嗎？我沒聽清楚。
> B：那你應該注意一點。

對話 二

A : Did you understand what the professor was explaining today?
B : I didn't get that at all.

> A：教授今天解釋的你聽的懂嗎？
> B：我一點也不懂。

## 加 強 練 習

| | |
|---|---|
| **repeat**<br>重複 | I'm sorry. Could you repeat what you said?<br>（對不起，請你再說一遍？）<br><br>I hope you won't repeat the same mistake again.<br>（我希望你不會又患同樣的錯誤。） |
| **pay attention to**<br>注意 | I didn't pay attention to what she said.<br>（我沒有注意她說的話。）<br><br>You should pay more attention to your kid.<br>（你應該多注意你的小孩。） |

☑ repeat     [rɪ'pit]     重複

☑ closer     ['klosɚ]     密切的

☑ attention     [ə'tɛnʃən]     名 注意；注意力

☑ professor     [prə'fɛsɚ]     教授

☑ mistake     [mə'stek]     名 錯誤

**Memo**

# 34 I don't care.

## 我不在乎

**輕鬆學** 當你說 I don't care. 這句話的時候,你是否自認為很瀟灑,可是要說這句話時,要注意到後果要自負的,瀟灑的結果,可能是丟到工作,老美小孩如果跟父母說這句話,可能遭到父母的嚴格訓誨。

如果是 I don't care for 某樣東西或事件,這句話就沒有「我不在乎」的意味,而是指你不喜歡那樣東西或事件,如果說 I don't care very much for 某樣東西或事件,意思就是「我不是很喜歡」那樣東西或事件。

## 對話 一

A : I don't care if I get in trouble with my boss. It's too nice a day to spend in the office.

B : That's not the proper attitude to have towards your job.

> A:我才不管我的老闆會不高興。今天這麼好的天氣不該待在辦公室裡。
>
> B:那不是你工作應有的態度。

## 對話 二

A : Do you think the Dallas Cowboys will ever reclaim the fame they had in the early nineties?

B : I don't care very much for football. I'm much more of a basketball fan.

> A：你認為達拉斯牛仔隊還能重振他們90年代初期的名聲嗎？
>
> B：我不是很喜歡足球。
>
> 我比較迷籃球。

## 加 強 練 習

| | |
|---|---|
| **attitude**<br>態度 | If you want to keep your job, you'd better change your attitude.<br>（如果你想保有你的工作，你最好改變你的態度。）<br><br>He has a good attitude towards his schoolwork.<br>（他對學校的功課有很好的態度。） |

| fan | I am a huge Mel Gibson fan. |
|-----|------------------------------|
| 迷  | （我是梅爾吉普森的大影迷。） |
|     | She's Sean Connery's biggest fan. |
|     | （她是史恩康納萊的大影迷。） |

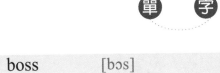

單　　字

| ☑ boss | [bɔs] | 名 主管；老闆 |
|--------|-------|--------------|
| ☑ spend | [spɛnd] | 動 花（時間） |
| ☑ proper | ['prɑpɚ] | 合適的 |
| ☑ attitude | ['ætətjud] | 名 態度 |
| ☑ towards | [tordz] | 對於 |
| ☑ reclaim | [rɪ'klem] | 恢復 |
| ☑ fame | [fem] | 名聲 |
| ☑ fan | [fæn] | （運動、電影等的）狂熱愛好者 |

# 35 I haven't got all day.

### 我可沒那麼多時間

**輕鬆學** 有人常常覺得一天 24 小時還不夠用,最好一天有 48 小時,總之,我們常常覺得時間不夠用,你說,哪裡還有時間用在等人呢,遇到有人拖拖拉拉,讓你等老半天,告訴他 I haven't got all day. 讓他知道你一整天的時間,還有很多其他的事要做呢,不可能把一整天的時間都用來等他。

## 對話 (一)

A : If you have something to say then say it.
   I haven't got all day.

B : I'm just trying to find the right words.

> A:如果你有話要說,就說。我可沒那麼多時間。
> B:我只是在找適當的用詞。

## 對話 二

A： Stop watching TV and help me to fix up the yard.

I haven't got all day to wait for you.

B： Just give me five more minutes.

> A：別再看電視了，來幫我整理院子。我可沒那麼多時間等你。
>
> B：再給我五分鐘。

## 加強練習

| help 幫忙 | Could you help me with my homework?（你可以幫忙我的家庭作業嗎？） |
|---|---|
| | Come help me fix up the yard.（來幫我把院子整理整理。） |

| **I'm just trying to....** 我只是試著要… | I'm just trying to help him make the right decision. <br> （我只是試著要幫他做正確的決定。） |
| | I'm just trying to make it up to you. <br> （我只是試著要補償你。） |

### 單　　字

| ☑ right | [raɪt] | 形 正確 |
|---|---|---|
| ☑ yard | [jɑrd] | 名 庭院；院子 |
| ☑ homework | [ˈhomˈwɝk] | 家庭作業 |
| ☑ decision | [dɪˈsɪʒən] | 名 決定 |

# 36 I'm not kidding.

我不是在開玩笑

輕鬆學 kid 這個字當動詞，可以做「開玩笑」的意思，遇到你認為很嚴肅的問題，你希望對方知道，就該提醒他一句 I'm not kidding.

**對話 一**

A : I'm not kidding.

You'd better take these suits to the dry cleaners today, or they won't be ready for the wedding on Saturday.

B : Don't worry so much.

I'll drop them off after lunch.

> A：我不是在開玩笑。你最好今天就把這些西裝拿去乾洗店，否則會趕不及星期六的婚禮。
>
> B：別擔心那麼多。我午飯後就會拿去乾洗店。

115

## 對話 二

A : I'm not kidding when I say that I don't want to see you ever again.

B : Oh come on.

Please give me another chance.

> A：當我說我不想再看到你時，我不是在開玩笑的。
>
> B：別這樣。
>
> 再給我一個機會嘛！

## 加 強 練 習

| You'd better.... 你最好 | You'd better hurry up, or you'll miss the bus.<br>（你最好快點，否則你會搭不上公車。） |
|---|---|
| | You'd better get up now.<br>（你最好現在就起床。） |

**Come on.**
別這樣

A : Sorry. You can't go.

B : Come on, let me go to the movies with her.

A：對不起，你不可以去。

B：別這樣，讓我跟她去看電影嘛。

| ☑ kid | [kɪd] | 開玩笑 |
|---|---|---|
| ☑ dry cleaner | | 乾洗店 |
| ☑ suit | [sut] | 西裝 |
| ☑ chance | [tʃæns] | 名 機會 |
| ☑ wedding | [ˈwɛdɪŋ] | 婚禮 |

# 37 I'm sorry to hear that.

### 聽到這消息我很難過

輕鬆學 有人跟你説，他遇到了不幸的事情，丟了工作，考試考不及格，家裡有人生病等等，你是否滿心關懷卻又不知如何安慰對方呢，老美聽到有人遇到不幸，第一句話一定是説 I'm sorry to hear that.

對話 一

A : You look down.

B : Yeah, my grandfather just passed away.

A : I'm sorry to hear that.

> A：你看起來很沮喪。
>
> B：是的，我的祖父剛剛過世。
>
> A：聽到這消息我很難過。

## 對話 二

A： My husband didn't get the promotion at work that he was hoping for.

B： I'm sorry to hear that.

I know you guys were counting on that pay raise.

> A：我先生沒有得到他希望的升遷。
>
> B：聽到這消息我很難過。我知道你們兩個等著那份加薪。

## 加強練習

| | |
|---|---|
| **down**<br>沮喪 | I feel a bit down today.<br>（我今天有一點沮喪。） |
| | He looks down. What's wrong with him?<br>（他看起來有點沮喪，他怎麼啦？） |

**count on**
當真

A : Mary said she would come to the party.

B : If I were you, I wouldn't count on her.

A：瑪麗說她會來參加宴會。

B：如果我是你，我不會把她的話當真。

☑ down       [daʊn]       形 心情不好

☑ pass away       去世

☑ promotion       [prə'moʃən]       升遷

☑ pay       [pe]       薪水

☑ raise       [rez]       動 加薪

# 38 That does it.

夠了

輕鬆學 是可忍孰不可忍，有些事情對方一做再做，已經到了你能夠忍受的極限了，該是你說 That does it. 的時候了，說了這句話，可得有後續的警語：你不能忍了。你將怎麼做呢，丟一些狠話，不過效果如何，可得看情形了。

## 對話 一

A : I almost forgot to tell you.
Mary called in sick this morning.

B : That does it.
She's missed too many days.
If she misses anymore, I'm going to have to let her go.

A：我差點忘了告訴你。瑪麗打電話來請病假。

B：我受夠了。她太多天沒來了。她如果再不來，我就要她走路。

## 對話 ○

A ： Mom, John says he's not coming home for dinner.

B ： That does it.
Tell your brother that he comes home for dinner with the family or else.

　　A：媽，約翰說她不回來吃晚飯。

　　B：我受夠了。告訴你哥哥，要他回來跟家人
　　　　一起吃晚飯，否則走著瞧。

## 加 強 練 習

| | |
|---|---|
| **miss**<br>錯過 | You'd better hurry up, or you'll miss the train.<br>（你最好快一點，否則你會錯過火車。） |
| | You can't take any days off anymore.<br>You've missed too many days.<br>（你不可以再請假了。你已經請太多天假了。） |

**forget**
錯過

He forgot to bring the lunch box with him.

（他忘了帶便當。）

She forgot to tell me she was not coming home for dinner.

（她忘了告訴我，她不回來吃晚飯了。）

| ☑ miss | [mɪs] | 動 錯過 |
|---|---|---|
| ☑ almost | [ˈɔl,most] | 幾乎 |
| ☑ forgot | [fɚˈgɑt] | 忘記（forget 的過去式） |
| ☑ else | [ɛls] | 其他的 |

# 39 Just a moment.

一會兒的時間

**輕鬆學** moment 這個字是的意思是「片刻的時間」，要請對方等 一會兒，就跟他説 Just a moment.，或者，屋裡的眾人玩鬧得很高興，也很大聲，你需要他們安靜一會兒，也就是請他們安靜 for just a moment.

**對話** 一

A : Can you keep the volume down for just a moment?

I'm on the phone.

B : Ok, we'll be quiet.

> A：你們可否小聲一點一會兒。我在講電話。
> B：好的，我們會安靜。

## 對話 ㈡

A : Have you seen my briefcase?

B : Just a moment, dear.

I can't hear you because I have the water running in the kitchen.

> A：你有沒有看到我的手提箱？
>
> B：請稍候。廚房裡的水在流著，我聽不到你說什麼。

## 加強練習

| | |
|---|---|
| **volume**<br>聲量 | Can you turn the volume of the TV down?<br>（你可以把電視機的聲量轉小聲一點嗎？）<br><br>I'll turn the volume of the TV up.<br>（我會把電視機的聲量轉大聲一點。） |

**run**
放水

I'll run you a hot bath.
（我去替你放一缸熱水。）

Who left the tap running?
（誰讓水龍頭開著？）

單　字

☑ volume　　['vɑljəm]　　音量

☑ quiet　　['kwaɪət]　　安靜的

☑ briefcase　　['brif͵kes]　　手提箱

☑ kitchen　　['kɪtʃən]　　廚房

☑ tap　　[tæp]　　水龍頭

# **40** Keep in touch.

保持聯繫

輕鬆學 　有人要搬離到他地去，有人要出遠門，你依依不捨，也希望他不要此去音訊全無，那就跟他叮嚀要 Keep in touch. 哦。Keep in touch. 的方法很多，可以寫信，可以打電話，現在的科技發達，不僅可以用 e-mail、line、WeChat、skype、facebook... 等視訊通話，還可以用 netmeeting，只要在電腦上裝 Webcam，不管對方到了地球上的哪個角落，你們都還可以彼此看到對方呢。

對話

A : I'm really going to miss you.

　　Don't forget to keep in touch.

B : Certainly.

A：我真的會想念你。別忘了保持聯繫。

B：我會的。

## 對話 二

A： I know that communications are not very convenient where you're going, but try to keep in touch.

B： I promise to call you as often as I can.

> A：我知道你要去的地方，聯絡不是很方便，但是要盡量保持聯繫。
>
> B：我答應你我會盡可能打電話給你。

## 加 強 練 習

| Don't forget... 別忘了 | Don't forget to turn off the light.（別忘了關燈。） |
|---|---|
| | Don't forget to bring the lunch box with you.（別忘了帶便當。） |

| promise<br>答應 | He promised to take me to the movies.<br>（他答應帶我去看電影。） |
| --- | --- |
| | He promised to help me with my homework.<br>（他答應要幫忙我的家庭作業。） |

| ☑ forget | [fɚ'gɛt] | 忘記 |
| --- | --- | --- |
| ☑ touch | [tʌtʃ] | 聯絡 |
| ☑ communication | [kəmjunɪ'keʃən] | 图 通信；聯絡 |
| ☑ convenient | [kən'vinjənt] | 形 方便的 |

# 41 Keep your chin up.

打起精神

**輕鬆學** chin 是「下巴」，人無精打采的時候，頭下垂，下巴
自然也跟著垂下去了，看到有人垂著頭，精神沮喪，
跟他說 Keep your chin up. 吧，遇到再大的事，只
要把 chin 抬高，精神一來，事情總是可以解決的。

**對話 一**

A : Losing one baseball game is not the end of
the world.

Keep your chin up.

B : I know you're right.

It's just disappointing.

> A：輸了一場足球可不是世界末日。打起精神來。
> B：我知道你說的對。只是很令人失望。

對話 二

A： Keep your chin up.

　　Don't let the bullies see you upset.

B： Ok, I'm trying very had to ignore them.

> A：打起精神來。
>
> 　　別讓那些惡霸看見你不高興。
>
> B：好的，我很努力試著不理他們。

加 強 練 習

| disappointing<br>令人失望的 | The result was quite disappointing.<br>（結果蠻令人失望的。） |
|---|---|
| | He brought us some disappointing news.<br>（他帶給我們一些令人失望的消息。）  |

| **ignore** | He ignored my question and went away. |
|:---|:---|
| 不理睬 | （他不理我的問題，就走掉了。） |

Try to ignore those bullies.
（盡量不要理那些惡霸。）

單　　字

| ☑ chin | [tʃɪn] | 下巴 |
|:---|:---|:---|
| ☑ disappointing | [ˌdɪsəˈpɔɪntɪŋ] | 令人失望的 |
| ☑ bully | [ˈbʊlɪ] | 惡霸 |
| ☑ upset | [ˈʌpˈsɛt] | 不高興 |
| ☑ ignore | [ɪgˈnɔr] | 不理 |
| ☑ result | [rɪˈzʌlt] | 名 結果 |

# 42 Keep your shirt on.

### 有耐心點

 我不知道為什麼叫人家有耐心點的英語，是跟他說 Keep your shirt on. 但這是一句很常見的英語，有人在趕你快一點，有人很不耐煩，有人緊張的希望他期待的日子快到，你都可以跟他說 Keep your shirt on.

**對話** 一

A : Where on earth is our bill?

We've been waiting a long time.

B : Keep your shirt on.

It's a very busy evening here.

> A：我們的帳單到底在哪裡？我們已經等了很久。
> B：有耐心點。今晚這兒生意很好。

133

## 對話 二

A : I can't wait until Friday.

Mary says she has a big surprise planned.

B : Keep your shirt on.

Friday won't come any faster.

> A：我等不及星期五到來。瑪麗說她計畫給我一個驚喜。
>
> B：有耐心點。你急，星期五也不會提早到。

## 加強練習

| | |
|---|---|
| **on earth**<br>到底 | When on earth do you expect me to come?<br>（你到底要我什麼時候來？） |
| | What on earth do you mean?<br>（你到底是什麼意思？） |

**busy**
忙的

I'm afraid John is busy at the moment. Can he call you back?

（我恐怕約翰正忙著。他稍後再打給你好嗎？）

I am afraid I can't meet you soon. I am busy the whole week.

（我恐怕沒有辦法很快跟你見面，我這個星期都很忙。）

單　字

| ☑ bill | [bɪl] | 名 帳單 |
| ☑ busy | [ˈbɪzɪ] | 忙的 |
| ☑ surprise | [səˈpraɪz] | 驚奇；驚喜 |

# 43 Knock it off.

停了吧

**輕鬆學** 宿舍裡隔室的人，喧嘩不已，吵得人不得安靜，過去跟他們説 Knock if off.；有人在你身旁緊張兮兮的踱來踱去，你也可以叫他 Knock it off.；你的好朋友被男朋友遺棄了，哭個不停，理論上你也可以叫她 Knocki it off. 但這樣做未免太不盡人情了吧，讓她哭個夠吧，總之，有人一直在做你不喜歡的事情，把你煩的要命時，你都可以叫他 Knock it off.

**對話** 一

A : You've been pacing around all afternoon. Knock it off.

B : I can't help it if I'm nervous.

A：你已經走來走去走了一個下午。別再走了。
B：我沒辦法，我很緊張。

136

## 對話 二

A： Why are you still crying?

Knock it off.

B： I can't help it if I'm a very emotional person.

A：你為什麼還在哭？別哭了。

B：我是一個很情緒化的人，這一點我也是沒辦法。

## 加 強 練 習

| | |
|---|---|
| **pace** **around** 踱步踱個不停 | Stop pacing around and sit down. （不要再踱個不停，坐下來吧。） |
| | There is no need to pace around. （沒有必要踱步踱個不停。） |

| **can't help it**<br>沒辦法 | I can't help it if she stands you up.<br>（她失約於你，我可是沒辦法啊。）<br>I can't help it if the baby keeps crying.<br>（嬰孩要哭個不停，我可是沒辦法。） |

單　　字

☑ pace around　　　　　　　　　　　踱步踱個不停

☑ nervous　　['nɝvəs]　　　　　緊張的

☑ emotional　　[ɪ'moʃənḷ]　　　感情的；情緒的

# 44 Let's call it a day.

**今天就到此為止。**

**輕鬆學** 一天 24 小時，什麼時候是一天終止的時候呢，以時間的觀念來説，應該是午夜 12 點吧，但是以人類的工作環境來説，要下班時，也就是宣告今天的工作到此告一段落，也好像是這一天可以到此為止，英語就説 Let's call it a day.

## 對話 一

A : Wow, do you realize that we've been here since 6:30 this morning?

B : You're right.

It is getting late.

Let's call it a day.

> A：哇，你們有沒有注意到，我們從今天早上六點就一直在這裡？
>
> B：你說的對。很晚了。今天就到此為止。

## 對話 〓

A： We've been trying to solve this problem for hours.

I think I'm getting too tired to think.

B： Let's call it a day and start fresh in the morning.

> A：我們已經花了好幾個鐘頭的時間，在想辦法解決這個問題。我想我已經想累了，沒辦法再想。
>
> B：今天到此為止，明早有精神再做。

## 加強練習

| It's getting...<br>天漸漸… | It's getting late.<br>（天漸漸晚了。） |
|---|---|
| | It's getting dark.<br>（天漸漸暗了。） |

| in the morning 明天早上 | I'll call him first thing in the morning. （明天早上我要做的第一件事就是打電話給他。） |
|---|---|

I'll finish my homework in the morning.

（我明天早上會把功課做完。）

單　　字

| ☑ late | [let] | 晚了 |
|---|---|---|
| ☑ solve | [sɑlv] | 解決 |
| ☑ problem | [ˈprɑbləm] | 問題 |
| ☑ fresh | [frɛʃ] | 新鮮的 |

# 45 Let's get together sometime.

我們有空要聚聚

輕鬆學 現代人都很忙，朋友間難得相聚，遇到你好久不見的朋友，跟他提議 Let's get together sometime. 吧，希望能得到對方善意的回應，忙裡偷閒，享受一下純友誼的閒聊吧。

對話 一

A : We don't see each other much outside of the office.

B : That's true.

Let's get together sometime.

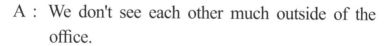

A：我們出了辦公室之後，就很少有時間在一起。
B：是啊。我們有空就聚一聚吧。

## 對話 二

A : I have to go and pick up the kids from soccer practice.

B : I haven't seen your family in a while. Let's get together sometime.

> A：我小孩在練習足球，我必須去接他們。
>
> B：我很久沒有看到你的家人了。有空我們就聚一聚吧。

## 加強練習

| each other<br>互相 | We had a lot to tell each other about the vacation.<br>（關於假期的事我們有很多要告訴對方。）<br><br>They were holding each other's hands.<br>（他們正手牽著手。） |
| --- | --- |

**pick up**
接

He promised to pick up the children after school.
（他答應放學後去接小孩。）

Can you pick me up at the airport?
（你可以來機場接我嗎？）

☑ outside     [ˈaʊtˈsaɪd]     外面

☑ true     [tru]     真的

☑ soccer     [ˈsakɚ]     足球

☑ practice     [ˈpræktɪs]     練習

# 46 **Look who's talking.**

### 烏鴉笑豬黑。

輕鬆學 如果有一天烏鴉開口笑豬黑的時候，你想豬聽了會很羞於自己長的這麼黑嗎？不會的，豬一定會大笑說道，唉呀，我還以為是誰在說話呢（who's talking），你看（Look）原來是一隻黑色的烏鴉在笑我黑，也不想想他自己不也一樣黑嗎？

## 對話 一

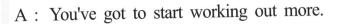

A : You've got to start working out more.

B : Look who's talking.

　　You're not exactly in the best of shape either.

> A：你應該開始都做一點運動。
> B：別烏鴉笑豬黑。你自己的身材也不是很好。

## 對話 ○

A： I have a friend who's a great family therapist. I think you might benefit from speaking with her.

B： Look who's talking.

Your family has its share of problems, too.

> A：我有一個朋友，他是家庭問題診療專家。我想你如果跟她談談，對你會很有助益。
>
> B：嘿，瞧你說的。你的家庭也是問題重重。

## 加 強 練 習

| | |
|---|---|
| **might** <br> 可能 | You might feel better if you take some medicine. <br> （你如果吃藥可能會覺得好些。） |
| | You might look better if you put on some make-up. <br> （如果你化妝一下，可能會好看些。） |

| either 也不 | You don't take a bath every night, either. <br> （你也是一樣沒有每天洗澡。） |
| --- | --- |
| | You are never on time, either. <br> （你也是從來都不準時。） |

**偷偷告訴你**

either 可以唸成 ['aɪðɚ]；也可以唸成 [iðɚ]。連美國人自己
都會一下唸 ['aɪðɚ]，一下唸 [iðɚ] 噢 !!

單　字

| ☑ exactly | [ɪɡ'zæktlɪ] | 確切的 |
| --- | --- | --- |
| ☑ shape | [ʃep] | 形狀 |
| ☑ therapist | ['θɛrəpɪst] | 治療專家 |
| ☑ benefit | ['bɛnəfɪt] | 受益 |
| ☑ medicine | ['mɛdəsn̩] | 醫藥 |
| ☑ make-up | ['mek‚ʌp] | 化妝品 |

# 47 Look who's here.

看誰來了

輕鬆學 你在宴會上偶然遇到一個好久不見的朋友，你會對著他說 Look who's here. 表示你沒期待會見到他，很驚喜。你也可以把他帶去見你們另一個共同的朋友，跟他說 Look who's here. 這是跟這個朋友說，你看看是誰來了，你相信他也會很驚喜看到你帶來的好久不見的朋友。

或者你帶了一個老朋友回家，跟老婆說 Look who's here. 這是在告訴老婆，我帶了一個朋友回來，你來看看是誰。

對話 一

A： Mary, look who's here.

B： John!

It's good to see you in town again.

> A：瑪麗，看誰來了。
> B：是約翰。很高興看到你來。

148

## 對話 二

A： Mary, look who's here.

I hope we made enough for dinner.

B： There's always enough for an old friend like Jenny.

A：瑪麗，你看誰來了。我希望我們晚飯夠請客。

B：給像珍妮這樣的好朋友，永遠是夠的。

## 加 強 練 習

| | |
|---|---|
| **in town**<br>來本地 | Come visit us when you are in town.<br>（如果你到本地來，要來看我們。）<br>------<br>Guess what? Jenny is coming in town.<br>（你猜猜看是什麼事？<br>珍妮要本地來。） |

149

**enough**
足夠

Have you made enough copies?
（你有沒有拷貝足夠的份數？）

Is there enough room for Mary?
（有沒有足夠的位置給瑪麗？）

☑ always    [ˈɔlwez]      總是

☑ enough    [ɪˈnʌf]      足夠的

☑ visit    [ˈvɪzɪt]      動 訪問；拜訪

☑ room    [rum]      空間

☑ town    [taʊn]      城市；城鎮

# 48 Lucky for you.

## 你真幸運

**輕鬆學** 這世上的事情，並非絕對公平，有人很幸運，你可以帶著羨慕的口吻跟他說 Lucky for you.，這句話也可以帶有「好在」的意思，表示壞事情雖然發生了，好在還沒有那麼嚴重。

## 對話 一

A : I just found out that Berkley University is giving me a football scholarship.

B : Lucky for you.

I have to work part-time to pay for college.

> A：我剛得知柏克萊大學要給我足球的獎學金。
>
> B：你真幸運。我得半工半讀來完成大學學業。

## 對話 二

A : Uh oh, I think I accidentally scratched my father's new Porsche.

B : Lucky for you that it's a black car and it's barely noticeable.

> A：喔噢，我想我不小心刮到我父親的新車寶時捷了。
>
> B：你還算幸運，這部車子是黑色的，刮一下幾乎看不出來。

## 加強練習

| work<br>part-time<br>做兼差 | Does he have a full-time job?<br>（他是全職工作嗎？） |
| --- | --- |
| | He only works part-time on the weekends.<br>（他只是在週末兼差。） |

| | |
|---|---|
| **barely**<br>幾乎不能 | He could barely recognize her.<br>（他幾乎認不出她來。）<br><br>We barely had time to catch the plane.<br>（我們幾乎來不及趕上飛機。） |

  單　字

| ☐ scholarship | [ˈskɑləˌʃɪp] | 獎學金 |
|---|---|---|
| ☐ pay | [pe] | 付錢 |
| ☐ barely | [ˈbɛrlɪ] | 副 幾乎不能 |
| ☐ scratch | [skrætʃ] | 刮痕；刮傷 |
| ☐ accidentally | [ˌæksəˈdɛntḷɪ] | 副 偶然地；意外地 |
| ☐ noticeable | [ˈnotɪsəbḷ] | 容易注意到 |

# 49 May I help you?

### 需要我幫忙嗎？

**輕鬆學** 如果你在商店逛來逛去，店員看到了，通常會問你
May I help you? 這句話含有，你需要什麼嗎的意
思，在美國，有一些韓國人開的小商店，當有老美進
來時，那些英語不怎麼好的韓國人會跟老美說 What
do you want? 他說這句話的意思，就是「你想要買
什麼東西」，或是「你要什麼東西」，但是老美店員
一定問說，May I help you?，所以有些老美認為韓
國店員說的話很衝，而起衝突，實際上，韓國人並沒
有惡意，他只是不曉得同樣的意思，英語應該怎麼說
而已。

## 對話 一

A： May I help you?

B： No thanks.

I'm just looking around.

A：需要我幫什麼忙嗎？
B：不需要。我只是四處看看。

154

對話 二

A : You seem to be a little lost.

　　May I help you?

B : Yes, can you tell me where Green St. is?

> A：你好像迷路了。需要我幫什麼忙嗎？
>
> B：是的，請告訴我格林街在哪裡？

加 強 練 習

| Can you tell me ....?<br>你能夠告訴我… | Can you tell me where the post office is?<br>（你能夠告訴我郵局在哪裡嗎？） |
|---|---|
| | Can you tell me why she is crying?<br>（你能夠告訴我她為什麼在哭嗎？） |

| **lost**<br>迷失 | I always get lost in big cities.<br>（我在大城市總是會迷路。）<br><br>It's getting late. They must have gotten lost.<br>（天漸漸晚了，他們一定是迷路了。） |

單　　字

☑ seem　　　　[sim]　　　　似乎

☑ lost　　　　[lɔst]　　　　迷路

☑ city　　　　['sɪtɪ]　　　　都市

☑ post office　　　　　　　郵局

# 50 My pleasure.

我的榮幸。

**輕鬆學** 大家學過的，有人謝謝你的幫忙，你就答說 You're welcome. 這是一句很標準也很通常的答法。你有時是不是會覺得能幫某人的忙，是你的榮幸，幫了他的忙，如果他跟你道謝，你就別說 You're welcome. 你可以回答 My pleasure.

## 對話 一

A : Thank you for bringing this up here.

B : My pleasure.

> A：謝謝你幫我拿這個上來。
> B：是我的榮幸。

## 對話 二

A : Thanks for helping with the garage sale.
　 I think we made a tidy profit.

B : It was my pleasure.

> A：謝謝你在我的車庫拍賣幫忙。我想我們賺了不少錢。
> B：是我的榮幸。

加 強 練 習

| | |
|---|---|
| **garage sale**<br>家庭二手拍賣 | I bought this beautiful lamp at a garage sale.<br>（我在家庭二手拍賣中，買了這個美麗的燈。）<br><br>We made $50.00 at the garage sale.<br>（我們搞了一個家庭二手拍賣，賣得 50 元。） |
| **Thanks for .....**<br>謝謝你 | Thanks for helping me with my homework.<br>（謝謝你幫忙我的家庭作業。）<br><br>Thanks for helping me wash my car.<br>（謝謝你幫忙我洗車。） |

| ☑ pleasure | ['plɛʒɚ] | 榮幸 |
| ☑ garage sale | | 在車庫拍賣東西 |
| ☑ tidy | ['taɪdɪ] | （口語）相當好的 |
| ☑ profit | ['prɑfɪt] | 名 利潤 |

**Memo**

## 51 Never mind.

算了

**輕鬆學** 你跟對方説了話，對方沒聽清楚，請你再説一遍，你如果覺得你剛剛説的話，沒什麼重要性，不想重複再説，你就可以回答他説 Never mind. 或是事情已經過去了，你不想再提，你也可以跟對方説 Never mind. 表示沒什麼重要的事，過去就算了。

**對話 一**

A : Could you repeat what you said?
    I didn't quite hear it.

B : Never mind.
    It wasn't important.

A：你剛剛說的話，再重說一遍好嗎？我沒聽清楚。
B：算了。沒什麼重要的。

**對話 二**

A : I know you asked me to do you a favor yesterday, but I completely forgot what it was that you needed?

B : Never mind.

I had someone else take care of it already.

> A：我知道你昨天要我幫你一個忙，但是我全忘了你需要什麼？
>
> B：算了。我已經找別人處理好了。

**加 強 練 習**

## Could you repeat what you said?
### 你可以再重說一次嗎？

Run that by me again.
（請再說一遍。）

What did you say?
（你剛剛說什麼？）

| | |
|---|---|
| **completely**<br>完全 | I've completely forgotten my appointment with her.<br>（我把跟她的約會全給忘了。） |
| | I've completely forgotten her telephone number.<br>（我把她的電話號碼全給忘了。） |

單　　字

☑ important　　　[ɪmˈpɔrtənt]　　　形 重要的

☑ favor　　　　　[ˈfevɚ]　　　　　（美語）幫忙；恩惠

☑ completely　　　[kəmˈplitlɪ]　　　完全地

☑ forgot　　　　　[fɚˈgɑt]　　　　忘記（forget 的過去式）

☑ appointment　[əˈpɔɪntmənt]　　　約會；約定時間

# 52 Nice talking to you.

## 很高興跟你聊天

> **輕鬆學** 在宴會上，不管你是跟認識或不認識的人聊天，聊過了，分手之前，你都可以跟對方說 Nice talking to you.，禮貌性的表示，剛剛跟你談話很愉快。

### 對話 一

A : We should get together more often.

B : I agree.

It was nice talking to you again.

> A：我們應該多聚聚。
> B：我同意。很高興有機會再跟你聊天。

### 對話 二

A : Well, I think I'm going to be off.

B : Nice talking to you.

> A：我想我該走了。
> B：很高興跟你聊天。

加 強 練 習

| | |
|---|---|
| **I think I'm going to...**<br>我想我要… | I think I'm going to take some days off.<br>（我想我要請幾天假。） |
| | I think I'm going to tell him the truth.<br>（我想我會告訴他事實。） |

| | |
|---|---|
| **often**<br>時常 | How often do you wash your dog?<br>（你多常洗你的狗？） |
| | I see Mary quite often.<br>（我常常與瑪麗見面。） |

☑ often      [ˈɔfən]      時常

☑ truth      [truθ]      事實

☑ quite      [kwaɪt]      非常

# 53 No kidding.

就是說嘛

**輕鬆學** kid 這個字可以做「開玩笑」的意思，天氣好熱，有人抱怨說這天氣好熱啊，你也正被熱的昏頭轉向的，聽到他的話，彷彿聽到知音之言，不禁回答他說 No kidding!，跟對方表示說，你說的確實不是開玩笑之語，這熱天氣我也是感同身受。

## 對話 一

A : I wish the economy would pick up already.

B : No kidding.

Many of my friends are currently unemployed.

A：我希望經濟趕快復甦。

B：就是說嘛！我有許多朋友都沒有工作。

## 對話 二

A : Have you noticed that a lot of fashions from the 60s and 70s are making a comeback?

B : No kidding.

Just the other day, I saw someone wearing bell-bottoms.

> A：你有沒有注意到很多 60 年代，70 年代流行的服飾又再流行了。
>
> B：就是說嘛！
>
> 前幾天，我看到有人穿喇叭褲。

## 加強練習

| **economy** 經濟 | The economy is in recession. （現在經濟不景氣。） |
| --- | --- |
| | I think the economy is improving. （我認為經濟在復甦。） |

| make a comeback 又重新流行 | Miniskirts are making a comeback. （迷你裙又再流行了。） |
| | Do you notice that bell-bottoms are making a comeback? （你有沒有注意到喇叭褲又再流行了？） |

| ☑ economy | [ɪˋkɑnəmɪ] | 經濟 |
| ☑ currently | [ˋkɝəntlɪ] | 目前的 |
| ☑ unemployed | [ˏʌnɪmˋplɔɪd] | 失業的 |
| ☑ notice | [ˋnotɪs] | 注意到；通知 |
| ☑ bell-bottoms | [ˋbɛlˏbatəmz] | 喇叭褲 |
| ☑ comeback | [ˋkʌmbæk] | 再度流行 |

# 54 No sweat.

沒問題

**輕鬆學** sweat 是「流汗」的意思，所做的事如果都不用流汗，那肯定是一件很簡單的事，有人要請你幫忙，你可以很爽快的回答他說 No sweat. 沒問題，小事一椿，這件事我做起來連汗都不用流就可以做好了。

**對話 一**

A : Do you think you can fix my car this weekend?

It's making funny noises.

B : No sweat.

I'm a very accomplished mechanic.

A：你想這個週末你能幫我把車子修理一下嗎？

車子跑起來有怪聲音。

B：沒問題。我是一個很好的技師。

對話 二

A : Do you think you'll be able to win the contest?

B : No sweat.

I've never been in better shape.

> A：你想比賽你會贏嗎？
> B：沒問題的。我現在是處在最佳的狀況。

加 強 練 習

| | |
|---|---|
| **funny**<br>奇怪的；有趣的 | The car is making a very funny noise.<br>（這車子有很奇怪的聲音。）<br><br>I really like talking to John. He makes really funny jokes.<br>（我很喜歡跟約翰講話，他講的笑話很有趣。） |

| **Do you think...** 你認為… | Do you think John can fix my computer? （你認為約翰可以修好我的電腦嗎？） |
| | Do you think he will win in the race? （你認為他比賽會贏嗎？） |

單　　字

| ☑ sweat | [swɛt] | 流汗 |
| ☑ funny | ['fʌnɪ] | 奇怪的 |
| ☑ noise | [nɔɪz] | 雜音 |
| ☑ accomplished | [ə'kɑmplɪʃ] | 熟練的 |
| ☑ mechanic | [mə'kænɪk] | 汽車修理工 |
| ☑ contest | ['kɑntɛst] | 图 比賽 |

170

# 55 No problem.

沒問題

**輕鬆學** 有人請你幫忙，或是有事找你商量融通，你如果認為可以答應的話，就答應的爽快一點，説 No problem.，別拖泥帶水的不爽快，你的好意對方反而不領情。

**對話 一**

A : I think I'm going to have to work late. Would you mind if we postponed our dinner plans?

B : No problem, I'll give you a call tomorrow.

> A：我想我會工作到很晚。如果我們的晚餐聚會延期的話，你會不會介意？
>
> B：沒問題，我明天會跟你打個電話。

對話 二

A : Do you mind if I carpool with you to work this week?

B : No problem.

> A：這個星期我跟你共搭一部車去上班，你介意嗎？
> B：沒問題。

加強練習

| **Would you mind....** <br> **你介意嗎** | Would you mind if I canceled our appointment? <br> （如果我把我們的約會取消掉，你介意嗎？） |

Would you mind if I smoked here?
（如果我在這裡抽煙，你介意嗎？）

| **carpool**<br>共搭一部車 | The other moms are trying to get a carpool together to baseball games.<br>（其他的媽媽們正試著安排小孩子共搭一部車去參加棒球比賽。）<br><br>I carpool with John to work.<br>（我跟約翰開一部車去上班。）<br><br> |

| ☑ postpone | [post'pon] | **動** 延期 |
|---|---|---|
| ☑ plan | [plæn] | 計畫 |
| ☑ carpool | ['kɑr‚pul] | 共搭一部車 |
| ☑ cancel | ['kænsḷ] | **動** 取消；中止 |

# 56 Not again.

別又來了

**輕鬆學** 你的朋友約翰老是出狀況，今天又有人來跟你説約翰打球時，不小心斷了手臂去住院，你一聽，怎麼又出狀況了，只好説 Not again.

你的母親一天到老嘮叨著，要你好好用功讀書，你今天一走出房門，想看一下電視，她又來問你怎麼沒在看書，看什麼電視，你覺得很煩，也可以滴咕的説 Not again. 只是這樣會很傷老母的心的，最好忍著點別説。

**對話 一**

A： I heard that Jimmy is in the hospital for a broken arm.

B： Not again.

He's always getting himself hurt in some way.

> A：我聽說吉米因為手臂斷了去住院。
> B：別又來了。他總是有辦法讓他自己受傷。

## 對話 二

A : Did you hear?

John was in another car accident yesterday.

B : Not again.

This is the third one this year.

A：你有沒有聽說了？約翰昨天又出車禍了。

B：別又來了。這是今年第三次了。

## 加強練習

**broken**
斷掉的

She went skiing and came home with a broken leg.

（她去滑雪，摔斷了腿回來。）

She fell off of the tree and got a broken arm.

（她從樹上摔下來，摔到了手臂。）

**accident**
意外事件

The accident happened at 5:00 a.m.

（這件意外事件在上午五點發生。）

She broke her arm in a car accident.

（她在車禍中斷了手臂。）

☑ broken     [ˈbrokən]     形 斷了

☑ arm     [ɑrm]     手臂

☑ hurt     [hɝt]     傷害

☑ accident     [ˈæksədənt]     名 意外事件；車禍

# 57 No way.

### 免談；不會的

**輕鬆學** 你上了一整天的班，累得半死，回到家，正想賴在沙發椅上休息一下子，結果老婆大人來了，說家裡面的糖用光了，要你出去買，你如果有膽量拒絕老婆大人的命令，就回答她 No way.，如果沒膽量拒絕，就乖乖的出去買吧。

No way. 還有另一種說法就是，表示「不會的、不可能的」的意思，大家約好要見面的時間到了，約翰卻還沒有出現，有人提出質疑，約翰是否把這次的約翰忘了，你知道約翰是最有責任的，絕不會忘了大家的約會，你也可以說 No way. 約翰不會忘記的。

## 對話 一

A : Tom, please run to the store and pick up some milk and eggs.

B : No way.

I spent 80 hours at the office this week. I deserve a break.

> A：湯姆，請你到商店跑一趟，買一些牛奶和蛋。
> B：免談。我這個星期上了八十小時的班。我需要休息。

## 對話 二

A : I don't see him yet.

Do you think he forgot about our appointment?

B : No way.

He's the most responsible person I know.

He's probably just caught in traffic.

> A：我還沒看到他。你想他會忘了我們的約會嗎？
> B：不會的。他是我認識最有責任的人。他可能遇到交通阻塞吧。

## 加 強 練 習

| | |
|---|---|
| **break**<br>休息 | I worked all day without a break.<br>（我工作一整天都沒有休息。）<br><br>Let's take a break.<br>（我們休息一下吧。）<br><br> |
| **traffic**<br>路上的交通 | The traffic seems very light today.<br>（今天路上的交通似乎不擠。）<br><br>I was stuck in heavy traffic for more than an hour.<br>（我被卡在繁忙的交通中超過一個鐘頭。） |

| ☑ run | [rʌn] | 跑步 |
| ☑ spent | [spɛnt] | 花費（錢或時間） |
| ☑ deserve | [dɪ'zɝv] | 動 應得 |
| ☑ break | [brek] | 名 短暫的休息 |
| ☑ responsible | [rɪ'spɑnsəbl̩] | 有責任的；負責的 |
| ☑ traffic | ['træfɪk] | 交通 |

**Memo**

# 58 Now you're talking.

### 你總算說了一句像樣的話

輕鬆學 ▶ 大家在聊天,通常都是言不及義的隨便聊聊,但是若有人所提的建議,或是所說的話,你覺得很中聽,例如:約翰提議要請大家去看電影,你趕快說 Now you're talking. 好像他剛剛講了半天的話,都好像沒在講話一樣,到了現在才開口講第一句話似的,事實是,你很高興聽到他說這麼一句話,剛才他說的話,你其實也沒有在注意聽。

## 對話 一

A : I'm starving.

Let's go get some lunch.

B : Now you're talking.

I thought we were never going to eat.

A:我餓死了。我們去吃午飯吧。

B:你總算說了一句像樣的話。我還以為我們就不去吃飯了呢。

## 對話 ⓶

A : I was thinking.

What if we take some of the money from marketing and put it into better R&D and improve the quality of our products.

B : Now you're talking.

Keep those good ideas coming.

> A：我在想。如果我們把一些用在行銷上的錢，拿去用在研發以改進我們產品的品質，怎麼樣。
>
> B：你總算說了像樣的話。繼續想一些好點子吧。

## 加 強 練 習

| | |
|---|---|
| **starve**<br>很餓 | Is dinner ready? I'm starving.<br>（晚餐好了沒有？我快餓死了。） |
| | Mary is starving herself to try to lose weight.<br>（瑪麗餓她自己，以想辦法減肥。） |

| What if ...<br>如果…，<br>你說怎麼樣 | What if we go to Europe instead of to New York.<br>（我們去歐洲而不要去紐約，你說怎麼樣？）<br><br>What if we don't cook and go out for dinner tonight.<br>（我們今晚不要煮飯，去餐館吃飯，你說怎麼樣？） |
| --- | --- |

單　　字

| | | | |
| --- | --- | --- | --- |
| ☑ starve | [starv] | 動 | 餓死；飢餓 |
| ☑ marketing | ['markɪtɪŋ] | | 行銷 |
| ☑ quality | ['kwɑlətɪ] | | 品質 |
| ☑ product | ['prɑdəkt] | | 產品 |
| ☑ improve | [ɪm'pruv] | | 改進 |

# 59 Run that by me again.

再說一遍

**輕鬆學** 當有人跟你說話，你沒有聽清楚，想請對方再說一遍時，較正式的說法是 Pardon me? 或是 Pardon?，或是直接了當的跟對方說 Would you repeat what you just said?，口語一點的說法是 Run that by me again.

**對話** 一

A : Did you understand the directions I just gave you?

B : Not really.

Can you run that by me again?

A：我剛剛給你說明，你有沒有聽懂？
B：不太懂。你能不能再說一遍？

## 對話 二

A： To set the machine, first plug it in, turn it on, adjust the settings and close the lid.

B： I'm sorry.

Run that by me again.

I wasn't paying attention.

> A：要設定機器，首先把插頭插上，開起來，把設定調好，然後把蓋子關上。
>
> B：對不起。再說一遍。我沒有注意聽。

## 加強練習

| directions
方向 | Let's stop and ask for directions.
（我們停下來問路吧。） |
| | Do you know the directions to the restaurant?
（你知道到飯店怎麼走嗎？） |

| | |
|---|---|
| **pay attention** 注意 | You should pay attention to what the teacher says.<br>（你應該注意老師說的話。）<br><br>He never pays attention to what I say.<br>（他從不注意聽我說什麼。） |

單　　字

☑ understand　[ˌʌndɚˈstænd]　　瞭解；明白

☑ directions　[dəˈrɛkʃənz]　　方向指示；說明

☑ machine　[məˈʃin]　　機器

☑ plug　[plʌg]　　插入插頭

☑ adjust　[əˈdʒʌst]　　動 調整

# 60 Suit yourself.

隨便你

> **輕鬆學** 你的好意，對方不領情，你是否覺得很洩氣，別洩氣，一句話 Suit yourself. 表示，我已經表達善意了，你不領情，就算了，suit 當動詞是「合適」的意思，這句話照字面的意思是「你就選擇適合你自己的去做」，美國人講著句話的意思是「隨便你了」。

## 對話 一

A : A few of us are headed to Tom's lake house for the weekend.

Want to come?

B : No thanks.

I think I have to work instead.

A : Suit yourself.

> A：我們幾個人這個週末，要到湯姆在湖邊的小屋。
>
> 　你要來嗎？
>
> B：不，謝謝你。我有工作要做。
>
> A：隨便你了。

## 對話 二

A : I've got extra tickets to the Boston Red Sox game on Friday.

Bring your wife and come along.

B : I'm sorry, but I already have plans.

A : Suit yourself then.

> A：我有多出來的波士頓沙克斯隊星期五的票。
>
> 帶你的太太一起來。
>
> B：對不起，但是我有其他的計畫。
>
> A：隨便你囉。

## 加強練習

| | |
|---|---|
| **head**<br>前往 | Where are you headed?<br>（你要去哪裡？） |
| | We are headed to a concert.<br>（我們正要去聽音樂會。） |

| come along 一起來 | A : We're going to May's cafe. Do you want to come along? |
| | B : Thanks, but I already have plans. |
| | A：我們正要去小美咖啡館，你要一起來嗎？ |
| | B：謝了，但是我有其他的事。 |

| ☑ instead | [ɪn'stɛd] | 不是 ... 而是 ... |
| ☑ suit | [sut] | **動** 合適 |
| ☑ lake | [lek] | 湖 |
| ☑ extra | ['ɛkstrə] | 額外的；多餘的 |
| ☑ concert | ['kɑnsɚt] | **名** 演奏會；音樂會 |

# 61 Sure thing.

當然了

**輕鬆學** 回答對方說「當然囉」，英語可以說 Certainly. 這個字就是當然的意思，語言絕不可能是千篇一律的，說法往往有很多種，所以，你要回答說「當然囉」，也可以說 Sure thing.

## 對話 一

A：Do you remember Jenny from college?
　　She's coming in town tomorrow.

B：Sure thing!
　　I haven't seen her in years.

　　A：你記得我們大學時的珍妮嗎？她明天要來我們這裡。

　　B：我當然記得她。我好幾年沒看到她了。

## 對話 二

A : I'll see you at the company picnic this year, right?

B : Sure thing.

I never miss it.

A：今年公司的野餐會上，我會見到你吧？

B：當然了。公司的野餐我從沒缺席。

## 加強練習

| in town 來本地 | I didn't know John was in town yesterday. （我不知道約翰昨天到本地來。） |
| --- | --- |
| | When do you expect Jenny to come into town? （你期待珍妮什麼時候到本地來？） |

| **miss**<br>錯過 | I never miss the company picnic.<br>（公司的野餐會我一定參加。）<br><br>I had the flu and missed her<br>birthday party.<br>（我患了流行性感冒，沒去參加她的的生日宴<br>會。） |

 單　字

☑ remember　　[rɪˈmɛmbɚ]　　記得

☑ company　　[ˈkʌmpənɪ]　　**名** 公司

☑ picnic　　[ˈpɪknɪk]　　野餐

☑ flu　　[flu]　　流行性感冒

# 62 Take it easy.

別急

**輕鬆學** 有人急的不得了，有人怒氣沖沖，趕緊跟他說 Take it easy. 別急，別急。easy 是「輕鬆」的意思，輕鬆的 take it，就是輕鬆的對待這件事，說這句話有緩和對方情緒的作用。

**對話 一**

A： I'm so nervous right now.
B： Take it easy.
Everything is going to be ok.

> A：我現在好緊張。
> B：別緊張。一切會沒事的。

**對話 二**

A： I always get butterflies in my stomach when I have to perform onstage.
B： Take it easy.
You'll do a great job.

> A：我每次要上台表演時，總是緊張的覺得要嘔吐。
> B：別緊張。你會做得很好的。

## 加 強 練 習

---

**nervous**
緊張的

I always feel nervous before an exam.

（每次考試前我都會很緊張。）

---

I was so nervous about my exams that I couldn't sleep.

（我好擔心考試，以致於睡不著覺。）

---

**perform**
表演

I am looking forward to seeing her perform.

（我期待著看她的表演。）

---

She performed very well at the piano concert.

（她在鋼琴演奏會上表現得很好。）

| ☑ nervous | [ˈnɝvəs] | 緊張的 |
| ☑ stomach | [ˈstʌmək] | 胃 |
| ☑ perform | [pɚˈfɔrm] | 動 表演 |
| ☑ onstage | [ɑnˈstedʒ] | 台上的 |

**Memo**

Memo

# PART 2

實用會話練習

# 1 What brings you to Taipei?

你為什麼來台北？

對話 一

**A** : Where are you from?
（你從哪裡來？）

**B** : I'm from Taiwan but I'm living in Texas.
（我從台灣來，但是我現在住在德州。）

**A** : How long have you lived in Texas?
（你在德州住多久了？）

**B** : About seven years.
（大約七年。）

**A** : Do you like it there?
（你喜歡德州嗎？）

**B** : For the most part, but I do miss my home.
（大致來說，我是很喜歡，但是我也會想家。）

對話 二

**A** : What brings you to Miami?

（你為什麼到邁阿密來？）

**B** : I'm on vacation.

（我在度假。）

I'm planning to visit several different states.

（我計畫到好幾州去看看。）

**A** : That sounds like fun.

（聽起來蠻有趣的。）

**B** : It has been so far.

（到目前為止是蠻有趣的。）

**A** : Well, tell me, what do you like most about your trip?

（告訴我，你旅遊中最喜歡的是什麼？）

**B** : I've met a lot of interesting people.

（我遇到許多有趣的人。）

加 強 練 習

How long have you lived in Texas?

（你在德州住多久了？）

Do you have any children?

（你有小孩嗎？）

Lovely day, isn't it?

（今天天氣真好，不是嗎？）

Is this your first visit to the States?

（這是你第一次到美國來嗎？）

What did you like most about your trip?

（你這一趟旅行，最喜歡的是什麼？）

What brings you to Taipei?

（你為什麼來台北？）

單　　字

| ☑ most | [most] | 大多數 |
| ☑ miss | [mɪs] | 動 想念 |

| | | |
|---|---|---|
| ☑ vacation | [vəˈkeʃən] | 名 休假；假期 |
| ☑ several | [ˈsɛvrəl] | 幾個 |
| ☑ different | [ˈdɪfərənt] | 形 不同的 |
| ☑ state | [stet] | 州 |
| ☑ trip | [trɪp] | 旅程；旅遊 |
| ☑ interesting | [ˈɪntrɪstɪŋ] | 有趣的 |

## Memo

# 2 What do you do for a living?

你做什麼為生？

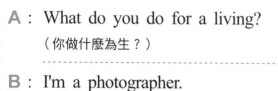

## 對話 一

**A :** What do you do for a living?

（你做什麼為生？）

**B :** I'm a photographer.

（我是個攝影師。）

**A :** Really? How interesting.

（真的？那多有趣。）

**B :** Well, I really enjoy it.

（嗯，我真的很喜歡攝影。）

## 對話 (二)

**A :** I just came back from Hawaii.

（我剛從夏威夷回來。）

**B :** Did you see anything interesting?

（你有沒有看到什麼有趣的事？）

**A :** Actually, I got to visit one of the volcanoes.

（事實上，我有機會去參觀了一座火山。）

**B :** Wow!

（哇!）

That sounds pretty cool.

（聽起來蠻好玩的。）

## 加強練習

What do you do for a living?

（你做什麼為生？）

Do you like doing that?

（你喜歡你的職業嗎？）

Is that a good job?

（那是個好職業嗎？）

How's your day been?

（你一天好嗎？）

Did you see anything interesting?

（你有沒有看到什麼有趣的事？）

☑ photographer [fə'tɑgrəfɚ]　　攝影師

☑ enjoy　　　　[ɪn'dʒɔɪ]　　享受；喜歡

☑ actually　　　['æktʃʊəlɪ]　　圃 實際上；事實上

☑ volcano　　　[ʌɑl'kenḷ]　　火山

☑ pretty　　　　['prɪtɪ]　　圃 非常；相當

# 3 Nice weather, isn't it?

天氣很好，不是嗎？

對話 一

**A** : What a beautiful day
（天氣真好。）.

**B** : It is nice.
（是很好。）

Especially the breeze.
（尤其是微風。）

**A** : I'm glad some of the hot weather is finally over.
（我很高興大熱天總算過去了。）

**B** : Me too.
（我也是。）

## 對話 二

**A**： Is it hot enough for you?

（這天氣夠熱了吧？）

**B**： No kidding.

（就是嘛。）

I'm burning up.

（我都快烤焦了。）

**A**： I know.

（我知道。）

I just wish it would rain.

（我只希望會下雨。）

**B**： Yeah, hopefully we'll get some by the end of the week.

（是啊，希望到了週末會有雨。）

## 加 強 練 習

Nice weather we're having.

（天氣真好。）

---

What a beautiful day.

（天氣真好。）

---

I wish it would rain.

（我希望會下雨。）

---

Is it hot enough for you?

（這天氣夠熱了吧？）

---

| ☑ weather | [ˈwɛðɚ] | 天氣 |
| --- | --- | --- |
| ☑ especially | [əˈspɛʃəlɪ] | 特別是 |
| ☑ breeze | [briz] | 微風 |
| ☑ finally | [ˈfaɪnl̩ɪ] | 最終；終於 |
| ☑ burn | [bɝn] | 燃燒 |
| ☑ hopefully | [ˈhopfəlɪ] | （口語）但願 |

## 4 What's up?

什麼事？

### 對話 一

A： Hey Mary!
（嗨，瑪麗。）

B： Oh, hey John.
（噢，嗨，約翰。）

What's up?
（有什麼事嗎？）

A： Nothing much.
（也沒什麼事。）

I was just thinking about going to the movies.
（我只是在想去看電影。）

B： What are you going to see?
（你想要去看什麼？）

**A：** I haven't really decided yet.

（我還沒真的決定。）

I'm just going to see what I feel like watching when I get there.

（我打算到了那裡看我喜歡看什麼。）

Do you like to watch movies?

（你喜歡看電影嗎？）

**B：** Yeah, I love movies.

（是的，我喜歡。）

**A：** Then why don't you go with me?

（那，你何不跟我一起去？）

**B：** Okay, sure.

（好啊。）

I'd love to go.

（我喜歡去。）

## 單　　字

| | | | |
|---|---|---|---|
| ☑ decide | [dɪˈsaɪd] | 動 | 決定；判斷 |
| ☑ movie | [ˈmuvɪ] | | 電影 |
| ☑ think | [θɪŋk] | | 想；認為 |
| ☑ really | [ˈrɪəlɪ] | | 真的 |
| ☑ feel | [fil] | | 感覺 |

**Memo**

# 5 What kind of movies do you like?

你喜歡什麼電影？

## 對話 一

**A** : What kind of movies do you like?
（你喜歡什麼電影？）

---

**B** : All kinds really.
（什麼電影都喜歡。）

---

But I especially like comedies.
（但是我特別喜歡喜劇。）

---

**A** : Yeah, I like comedies too and so does John.
（是啊，我喜歡喜劇，約翰也喜歡。）

---

But my favorite movies are horror flicks and art films.
（但是我最喜歡的電影是恐怖片和藝術電影。）

---

**B** : I've never really seen any art films.
（我沒真的看過什麼藝術電影。）

---

**A：** Not everybody likes them.

（不是每個人都喜歡藝術電影。）

They can be pretty strange.

（藝術電影有時候很奇怪的。）

If you'd like, you can come watch some of mine.

（如果你喜歡，你可以來看一些我的。）

**B：** Yeah, I'd like to check them out.

（好啊，我想去看看。）

**A：** No problem, you can come tonight if you want.

（沒問題，如果你想要，你可以今晚來。）

But I'm warning you, they're not for everyone.

（但是，我警告你，不是每個人都會喜歡。）

Most people don't care for them at all.

（大多數人都不喜歡。）

## 單　字

| | | |
|---|---|---|
| ☑ kind | [kaɪnd] | **名** 種類 |
| ☑ especially | [əˈspɛʃəlɪ] | 特別是 |
| ☑ comedy | [ˈkɑmədɪ] | 喜劇 |
| ☑ favorite | [ˈfevərɪt] | 最喜歡的 |
| ☑ horror | [ˈhɔrɚ] | 恐怖 |
| ☑ flick | [flɪk] | （口語）電影 |
| ☑ film | [fɪlm] | 電影 |
| ☑ strange | [strendʒ] | 奇怪 |
| ☑ warn | [wɝn] | 警告 |

**6** **What do you think of action films?**

你認為動作片怎麼樣？

對話 一

A： What do you think of action films?
（你認為動作片怎麼樣？）

B： Well, actually I like them.
（事實上，我喜歡動作片。）

Especially when they have good special effects.
（特別是有特技效果的。）

A： I saw a movie the other night that had great special effects.
（前晚我看了一部電影，有很棒的特技效果。）

I've still got it at the house if you want to borrow it.
（電影還在我家，如果你想看可以借去看。）

**B：** Yeah, I'd like to check it out.

（好的，我想看看。）

Maybe I'll get a chance to watch it this weekend.

（或許這個週末我會有機會看。）

**A：** I could bring it for you tomorrow.

（我明天可以帶來給你。）

**B：** Thanks, I'd like that a lot.

（謝謝，那很好。）

| | | |
|---|---|---|
| ☑ action film | | 動作片 |
| ☑ special | ['spɛʃəl] | 形 特別的 |
| ☑ effect | [ɪ'fɛkt] | 名 效果 |
| ☑ chance | [tʃæns] | 名 機會 |

# 7 Did you like the movie?

你喜歡那部電影嗎?

對話 一

A : Sorry I couldn't go to the movies with you.
（對不起，我沒辦法陪你去看電影。）

B : That's okay.
（沒關係。）

A : Did you have to go alone?
（你自己一個去嗎？）

B : No, actually Mary went with me.
（沒有，事實上，瑪麗跟我一起去了。）

A : What'd you go see?
（你們去看什麼？）

B : We went to see The Lord of the Rings but it was sold out.
（我們本來要去看魔戒，但是票賣光了。）

So, we saw some silly comedy instead.

（所以我們就看了一部很蠢的喜劇片。）

---

A： Did you like it?

（你喜歡那部電影嗎？）

---

B： Yeah, it was pretty good.

（喜歡，還蠻好看的。）

---

It was kind of dumb but it was funny.

（有一點蠢，但是蠻好笑的。）

---

You know I like comedies so I didn't mind.

（你知道我喜歡喜劇片，所以還好啦。），

---

A： That's cool.

（那很棒。）

---

I wish I could've gone but I was so busy.

（我希望我能去，但是我真的很忙。）

---

B： Yeah, I understand.

（是的，我瞭解。）

---

But hey, we're going to the movies again next weekend.

（但是，我們下個週末還要去看電影。）

- - - - - - - - - - - - - - - - - - - - - - - - - - - - - - - - -

Do you think you can come then?

（你想你能來嗎？）

- - - - - - - - - - - - - - - - - - - - - - - - - - - - - - - - -

**A**： I'll try my best.

（我盡量看看。）

- - - - - - - - - - - - - - - - - - - - - - - - - - - - - - - - -

**B**： You do that because I really want you to come.

（你盡量吧，因為我真的希望你來。）

- - - - - - - - - - - - - - - - - - - - - - - - - - - - - - - - -

☑ alone   [ə'lon]    形 單獨的；獨自

☑ silly   ['sɪlɪ]    傻的

☑ dumb   [dʌm]    形 愚笨的

| ☑ funny | [ˈfʌnɪ] | 奇怪的；滑稽 |
| ☑ mind | [maɪnd] | 動 介意 |
| ☑ busy | [ˈbɪzɪ] | 忙的 |
| ☑ understand | [ˌʌndɚˈstænd] | 瞭解；明白 |
| ☑ try | [traɪ] | 嘗試 |

**Memo**

國家圖書館出版品預行編目資料

輕鬆學會美國口語/蘇盈盈著. -- 新北市：哈福企業有限公司, 2021.06
面； 公分. -- (英語系列；72)

ISBN 978-986-06114-3-4(平裝附光碟片)

1.英語 2.口語 3.會話

805.188 110008929

英語系列：72

書名 / 輕鬆學會美國口語
作者 / 蘇盈盈
出版單位 / 哈福企業有限公司
責任編輯 / Jocelyn Chang
封面設計 / Lin Lin House
內文排版 / Co Co
出版者 / 哈福企業有限公司
地址 / 新北市板橋區五權街 16 號 1 樓

電話／ (02) 2808-4587
傳真／ (02) 2808-6545
郵政劃撥／ 31598840
戶名／哈福企業有限公司
出版日期／ 2021 年 6 月
定價／ NT$ 330 元（附 MP3）
港幣定價／ 110 元（附 MP3）

全球華文國際市場總代理／采舍國際有限公司
地址／新北市中和區中山路 2 段 366 巷 10 號 3 樓
電話／ (02) 8245-8786 傳真／ (02) 8245-8718
網址／ www.silkbook.com 新絲路華文網

香港澳門總經銷／和平圖書有限公司
地址／香港柴灣嘉業街 12 號百樂門大廈 17 樓
電話／ (852) 2804-6687 傳真／ (852) 2804-6409

email ／ welike8686@Gmail.com
網址／ Haa-net.com
facebook ／ Haa-net 哈福網路商城
Original Copyright © AA Bridgers, Inc. USA

哈福